DEVIN's
01: Eterna
– By
J P Kirk

barbintosh BOOKS

– Dedication & Thanks –

*To those who have left your indelible marks on my heart;
with love, I thank you.*

You know who you are!

My special thanks go to Deborah Murrell for your patience with the edit; Claire Rushbrook for the proofread; and to my family, friends, and fellow authors, whose exhortation keeps making these things happen.

– PROLOGUE –

100 years from now
PARIS

Marc Devin is naked save for a small towel around his waist. Staring out of the hotel window, he watches a stratotranscender lift from Charles de Gaulle Spaceport, and climb steadily into space.

A magenta sky heralds sunset. The murmuring newsfeed distracts with a piece about that autopod accident, in the city. The one where four Parisians lost their lives the other day. They're saying it was terrorists, but Devin knows better.

His jaw clenches at the thought of what's to come. He struggles to control his emotions.

I don't want to go back into space. I hate it, after what happened last time. Who in all of the hells actually wants to be out there, anyway?

He turns to regard himself in the mirror. A stranger stares back.

Who the hells are you? The nose doesn't look right, the jaw-line's way off…and this cheap link they've planted at my temple, ensnaring me with the rest of the herd…I look like one of those tech-heads now, addicted to the link. Only one with an axe to grind.

His head aches because of it, one of the few born with a natural hypersensitivity.

He's aware his new masters will be keeping close tabs on him, for sure. Even with the temporal device dialled to its most subtle level, the link would keep him forever immersed; an unwilling part of a virtual world orchestrated by AI, but connected to *them*. Marc Devin is in the employ of Bureau09, the secretive department supposedly protecting the interests of Europa-State, across all the colonies of the solar system.

He allows himself a fleeting recollection of his former life, a moment shared with Jenn.

She was so beautiful. I thought we really had something. Why did the crazy bitch have to do what she did?

He steels himself for the consequences, his link sure to catch these wayward thoughts. In punishment, it issues nerve impulses, signals that twist his innards painfully in the Bureau's 're-orientation', known as 'intestoration'.

He bends in agony.

Gods, any of you who might be listening...it hurts. But just another few seconds, nearly through it...

He gasps as it stops, he tended to hold his breath during intestorations.

He forces a degree of calm by moving slowly. He picks up the glass of synthetic mini-bar whisky he's been nursing since showering and takes a gulp. The cheap liquid burns his throat and makes him feel giddy. Out of disgust he slams it against the wall. Fragments tinkle to the synthetic flooring.

They can bill me. I won't find my answers at the bottom of a bottle; at least that's something.

He steadies himself on the windowsill, and contemplates his reflection again.

Harsh resentment bubbles to the surface once more. He trembles, the nerve-induced intestoration returns as his thoughts turn to the subversive. His link fights to control his train of thought.

It usually wins.

He needs to vent his rage. An idea comes to him. He reaches down and picks up a shard of the unfortunate glass, eyeing it curiously.

His loins stir.

Why it is making me feel like...like this?

He presses the shard against his forearm. With a smooth but spiteful stroke, he leaves a superficial cut. His mood takes a melancholy turn and he cuts vindictively because of...*something,* again and again.

6

He looks about himself, guiltily.

It doesn't make the crushing pain go away. Nor does it soothe the fierce ache in the pit of his stomach, or the eternal headache he suffers. But it does feel like some kind of outlet. A sense of the perverse deepens, he gets an erection.

Gods – any one of you – what have they reduced me to? Just look at yourself. You're getting a hard-on cutting yourself!

Guilt wraps round him, like a claw. Feeling suddenly ashamed, he tosses the shard of glass away and it clinks back to the ground. He feels revulsion at what those bastards have driven him to. What's left of his pride demands *why* he should have to self-destruct like this?

Come on, you're better than this.

But the erection doesn't go away.

His tormented mind drifts to that attractive receptionist who checked him in. Tingling in his loins returns; he wants sex.

Yeah, she was nice, kind of arse you can get lost in forever.

He imagines stalking and taking the unsuspecting girl roughly, letting her feel just what the universe has done to him.

She'd show me pity. For what Jenn has done. Losing Raquel. How Moray used me, how the Bureau ensnared me in all this! Yes, she'd be sorry for it all, and –

Something in him thinks twice.

I haven't descended to rape. They can't drive me to that, not yet they can't!

The line between right and wrong blurs, almost as though it's not even there. A subjective point of view to twist whichever way the wind blows.

The urge for sexual assault subsides, but he can't resist thinking again of Jenn. His former life. A tear rolls down his face; he feels utterly trapped like a bested animal. Helpless, with no-one to turn to.

He grieves for a time he knows he'll never see again, for a status society will never afford him, once lost. His body yearns for things to be so very different to the way they are now...

Gods, if only life had a reset button.

1

RELUCTANCE

Some months earlier
LONDON

The more senior gentleman had his eyes closed; it was late. In the physical sense he was stretched out in his plush white office, but his mind was elsewhere, entirely.

His surgically fitted, temporal implant had him immersed in a fantasy world, not too far removed in fact from the real one he inhabited, only older, more traditional. Perhaps he lacked imagination, but he was content to have the same furniture arrangement, the window, the door all in the same positions as his office, *in the real.*

Despite his Spartan tastes he rather fancied himself as Lord of the Manor, therefore in this fantasy world he came across that way. Replete in Harris tweed with mahogany panelling enveloping his green leather...throne, which was the only way to describe the enormous, gilt-edged chair behind his marble desk.

Sophisticated AI – and lots and lots of processing power – fed his mind this direct simulation. So, when his hand brushed the old-style paper on his desk, it felt even more real than real; smells, sounds and every sensation were uncannily reproduced and augmented, sweetened. When he breathed, he could smell the mahogany panelling, he could take in the frowsy aroma of the leather-bound volumes lining the walls, he could sense the particulates in the air from the glowing pipe he'd put out, just moments ago.

Although he was quite pleased with himself in his modestly indulgent surroundings, he wasn't alone. The grey figure sat opposite remained an indecipherable blur, the way they wanted it; in fact, he had never actually seen the face of his controller, never mind ever having had the pleasure in the flesh, as it were.

The pair didn't exactly converse, not in the traditional sense. Their exchange was made up of gestures, vague utterances and symbols floating back and forth across the desk, an essential encryption to which only they themselves were privy. But he calmly absorbed the information, analysed, evaluated and drew conclusions at a steady rate.

The exchange went on for some time; evidently he was less than pleased with his conduct the last time. There was the question of a considerable sum, still unaccounted for. But the compelling fact was that their organisation had to act quickly to ensure they were best placed to exploit a forthcoming opportunity, and he was charged with doing just that. Further investigations would be pending the outcome of this assignment, and if he balls'd this one up as well…

He pondered the fact that he would have to move several other pieces around to accommodate his plan, but via a complex pattern of sweeping hand gestures and grunts he was able to convince him that he would be up to the challenge, and the endeavour would be as copper-bottomed as one could ever hope. Yes, it would take some doing but, with some subtleties and applied pressure, he was able to convey the merit in his plan.

The case for action was clear, and he felt energised to move fast, to move his sleeper-operative into place quickly. For time was of the essence.

*

SWITZERLAND

Claudette Lambert held the man's head against the door frame of his office, and pushed harder.

'Who is the project assigned to?'

She didn't express the words, not verbally. It was a direct-send, from her link to his.

"I-I don't know." Snot spouted from the man's nose. "They wouldn't tell me."

The small, athletic woman exerted further pressure, then a little more, until his skull *clicked.* A prelude to fracture.

The man shrieked. "Gods, you're hurting me!"

'I shan't ask again.'

"Honestly, I, I –"

Claudette pushed harder, and something crunched. Physically, she was hooded, in the darkness. In the immersive sense, she was less than a fleeting shadow, an active layer of her clothing masking her online presence. Her victim never knew what hit him.

"You're hurting me!"

'I will not stop.'

"Okay, Okay. I assigned it to Patton. In R&D…in Zug."

'The whole thing? Or only parts?'

"All of it. That's it, I swear!"

Claudette loosened her grip, and struck the man at the base of his skull. He crumpled like a rag doll, to the ground.

So, she knew where the bounty would be; that would please her superiors. They'd just called her into action, and they could always rely on Claudette Lambert for a speedy, efficient job.

*

LONDON

It was the fact he couldn't sleep that kept Peter Hubbard awake.

Today's presentation weighed heavily, his mind a restless ape grasping at one worrisome branch after another. The crush of what could go wrong, *would* go wrong, and the professor's inevitable reaction if he screwed up.

What bothered him most was if he lost it all, lost her. In this life, status was everything.

A good sleep would help; gods, he'd been telling himself that, over and over, these past six hours. *It'll be ok. I've been before the board a few times now, no problem! So the old fart or one of those other derelicts will grandstand, belittle me? Pah! If I can't answer, I'll stall them 'til Mal can figure it out. Easy! Maybe not so easy...*

His mind was having none of it. He had a vision of being on the receiving end of a very thorough kicking, the door marked exit and a future doomed to solitude shovelling shit amongst the proletariat.

He felt for her to his left, his erection making a tent in their bed clothes. He couldn't help himself, the damned thing seemed to have a mind of its own. It seemed only one of two things was going to make it go away; but, still irked at the way she'd been last night. Peter rose to pee instead.

His mouth tasted horrible. Like something had died there, re-animated, then died all over again. He pulled on his robe and padded clumsily out of their tiny rest space. Entering the compact wet-space, he murmured 'breakfast, bright', and relieved his swollen bladder. This morning's oatmeal would be blended with a dose of the mild stimulants.

He squinted as he entered the dining space. "Softer, Summer, softer."

The domestic AI obliged by lowering the already unobtrusive lighting a degree further. The coruscating moodwall retracted in sympathy.

Peter scratched at his mussed umber hair and yawned. He took the black Colombian blend and oatmeal game-fully prepared by their manufactarium, and settled on to a stool that morphed to take his weight.

Eyes half-closed, he stirred absently at his rich-smelling breakfast. He wondered if he didn't deserve a treat this morning, on such an important day.

Especially seeing as I didn't sleep properly last night, either...

12

Like a magnet polarising his mood suddenly, self-indulgence got the better of him. He leant over to a wall unit and retrieved what remained of his last tube of real bee's honey.

'Peter…' chided Summer softly. She laboured constantly keeping him to the calorie-controlled lifestyle she'd set him.

"Just one last time," he rationalised, more to himself than the AI. He tossed the empty tube into a receptacle and their tiny manufactarium began recycling it for constituent parts.

Peter had brought Summer's source code with him after graduation, a couple of years back. He'd told himself he didn't want all that hassle affiliating a new AI, but his girlfriend had come to know better.

Although she'd only moved in recently, Jenn had been quick to berate his symbiosis with the AI; "She reminds me of old Nanny, Summer. She was our mother-hen as well, growing up. Constantly clucked around us too, she did. Like that AI does with you. Does she wipe your arse as well?"

So the name had stuck.

Peter stretched. "News."

A 3D holo sprang into the air from the infopanel, before him. Summer made sure the projection glowed and throbbed in direct sympathy with his mood. He flicked tiredly through a number of menus, looking for his favourite newsfeed.

'It would be more efficient if you just linked with the news, Peter. I can treat the bad head it gives you, with soothes.'

He tried to ignore the AI. Normally it didn't annoy him this much having his 'old school' methods called into question like this. He was edgy, grumpy. Un-slept and dreading the day ahead.

'You'll see it isn't due to rain all day today,' Summer continued, rejudging her interaction with him, *'but they'll still be raising the flood barrier. Third time this week already, to assist in draining the Thames basin. You'll be able to see it at 4pm if you look east, along the river.*

13

There's also another viral outbreak emanating from Pan-Asia, so watch your personal hygiene.'

Peter tuned her out, and flicked past the articles in question.

But Summer was still game. *'And the terrorists have been active again, so you should take extra care today. That's the second time this week they've tried to bomb London Galactic, Heathrow. Shocking, isn't it?'*

His attention settled on to a murmuring article about Esperanza City. His voice was little more than a murmur. "I see they're having to double the number of 'climate refugees' they're accepting down in New Greenlands, Antarctica. Good. We've bid for prime contractor; that should get me points from the board, for my new system."

'I agree. Your fledgling DZ climate management system is a miracle of engineering. It's only right they recognise it as such.'

"Should get a nice status boost, too."

'Indeed. And very well deserved, I might add.'

The article continued, reporting on the human factor. The many lives lost making the treacherous journey from the southernmost tip of the United States of the Americas, to the more temperate parts of the South Pole. His eyelids grew heavy.

A *bump-thump* and rustling caught his attention, coming from their rest space.

Peter looked over at the connecting doorway and eventually she emerged. Jenn's eyes were half closed, and she was scratching absently at her head as she shuffled in.

He wondered what had woken her. But he certainly knew better than to attempt any form of exchange at that very moment.

Let her get over the hump, first. She doesn't do mornings.

He tried to not look too obvious as he watched her take her coffee silently from the manufactarium. Jenn settled wordlessly opposite him.

14

Her rust coloured hair framed her face, freckled as though an artist had flicked a brush. She cradled the glass of black liquid, letting the steam rise into her narrowed eyes.

Her voice was a near whisper. "You really should link, Peter... like the rest of humanity. Embrace the simple notion of *direct-send*."

The sarcasm heaped on to that last remark irritated him. But he knew he was in real trouble, because she'd used his first name.

Yikes.

She sniffed. "I can hear you reviewing that crappy old newsfeed every morning, you know."

"I didn't realise I'd engaged audio, sorry. Besides, immersing gives me headaches, you know that."

She took a long draw of her Colombian blend and visibly straightened. Her temporal link worked hard waking her. This technological crutch Peter had never been able to rely on, thanks to being one of a tiny minority suffering the dreaded 'immerser's curse'.

"Well, I hope there was something interesting on there for you to look at." Her tone was condescending, her eyes finally settling on to him. But it seemed her link was doing a sterling job guiding her through her startup routine.

"Not particularly." He tried to sound nonchalant, but it actually sounded more *petulant.*

"I don't know why you're so fascinated with those newsfeeds anyway. It's always bad news, whichever way you cut it. By direct-send or through that antique crystal ball, the way you do."

He let the insult slide. "Not necessarily. There was a piece on there just now relating directly to my work. Should be *very* good news. For us, I mean. Plus I read last night they're tightening up on link regulations again, permissible limits on full immersion and all that stuff. Which, in my opinion, can only be a good thing."

"Yay."

"You sound thrilled."

15

"I can't get juiced about yet more restrictions. You don't understand, you don't like immersing. But for those of us who do, who're actually *living* in this century and not shackled to artefacts from the past," she gestured at the infopanel and his 3D holo, "it means a great deal. They're already stopping us staying deep very long these days, and you say it's gonna get worse? All because a few tech-heads out there can't keep their grip on reality. Well, I say, screw them."

"It's worse than that, Jenn, and you know it. It's actually quite chilling. Those poor people would rather stay immersed, and let their bodies wither and decay, than face what society has become."

"Here we go again. You're just so out of touch, Peter. Okay, so the world's a crappy place, I get it. Over-populated, half of which are refugees and lunatics trying to bomb us into gods-know-what, while over here it never stops peeing down. Can you wonder why so many of us long for an escape? It's not my fault there are a few weaklings out there, proles the lot of them, I bet you. Parasites who can't even lift their sorry arses out of their pits, let alone fend for themselves. So I have to suffer because of their decrepitude? Screw them. I can handle myself, linked-in."

"It's more than just a few, Jenn. There are thousands – *millions* worldwide. And it's getting worse. It's becoming a pandemic. And you're hardly a casual user yourself, are you?"

She glared at him. "Don't. This is one subject that'll always divide us, my love. Mainly because you don't immerse, you simply don't understand what it's like in the link. How liberating it is. How much *better* than real life it truly is."

"Aw, gee, thanks."

She smirked.

But Peter was still quite serious. "That's the point though, isn't it? It worries me. I'm seeing a *bona fide* zombie apocalypse right here, before my own very eyes. Realer-than-real, yeah, I've heard all the hype. So, you'd rather be frolicking in fantasyland than engage with the actual people around you? It's getting worse by the second; nobody has time for anybody these days."

"You're just an old fart living in the past. You can't stem the flow of progress."

He bit his tongue. She was goading him. "I can't be an old fart. I'm still in my twenties."

"Only just." A hint of a smile grazed her face, but her eyes remained icy. "Anyway, I think you were born middle-aged. And immerser's curse is just your perfect excuse."

He shook his head and let it go. A variation on this same argument was what sparked their row last night. And for some reason, he suddenly didn't have it in him to fight back this morning.

He pecked at his bright oatmeal and she sipped at her rich 'Colombian' coffee, which had in fact been grown atop their complex, in the Skygarden. The stuff was just about as Latin-American as a London red bus.

"Are we going to get any Sun today?" She put down her empty glass.

"Perhaps the odd glimpse or two." He tried to sound cheerful. "At least it's not going to rain all day, anyway."

She sneered only half-jokingly. She really hated the rain.

He gazed at her.

Jenn had an oval face, so tiny it made her hazel eyes seem *huge*. Her broad nose was not complimented by her thin lips however, and this made her features seem heavier than they really were.

"I had a dream last night I was being screwed by a dozen men." Her eyes widened suddenly, taking Peter utterly by surprise. "They were quite rough, and they ravished me. But they were all so very, very thorough. Mmmm..."

Almost choking on his breakfast, he could barely raise an inquisitive eyebrow. "You know, it astounds me sometimes just how unpredictable you can be."

"When I woke up, I wanted sex but you weren't there." She slid off the chair. Her robe opened to reveal one of her smooth thighs. "But you're here now, aren't you?"

She put her arms around his neck. Her eyes were bright and shining now, her link replaying vivid memories of the dream in real-time.

Fearing he had little choice but to surrender to her desires, he steadied himself.

She kissed round his neck. "You were up early. Trouble sleeping?" Despite the words, her tone conveyed a cold disinterest.

"Yes, my body wanted to sleep but my stupid brain was having none of it." He tried to not sound too self-indulgent. "I've got quite a big day today, have I not?"

He paused for a reaction, but she said nothing.

"The presentation to the board this morning," he explained at her blank expression. "Gods Jenn, I've been telling you about it for over a *week*."

Her immersed mind wasn't really taking it in, or perhaps she simply didn't care. He would never truly know.

Her eyelids fluttered, and she looked far away as her link stoked her sex drive. She pushed hungrily against him, pressing her groin into his.

Somehow Peter felt detached from the experience.

I'm just a vessel, the nearest actual male. Those deep eyes seem dead inside. Does she really want me?

But he did know she was inexorably committed to a certain path, and nothing in the universe would stop her now. So, his only option was to brace himself, and enjoy the ride.

She kissed him, her eyes staring coldly into his. She breathed hard as her tongue rushed in search of his…

If only I could immerse, share some of this dream spurring her on. Gods, we'd have one heck of a ride.

18

But right now, Peter had to admit his primary concern was to just hold on.

She unfastened his robe before parting hers, mounting him. His stool hastily bolstered itself, adapting to their combined weight.

Without a word, she made love to him there and then in the dining space.

*

"Space?" Peter Hubbard's incredulity showed.

His mentor, Professor Gerard Moray, nodded. "You'll be testing your prototype aboard Berthold Beitz space facility, in low Earth orbit. Congratulations."

"Surely there must be some mistake."

"No mistake."

"But why send me, sir? With all due respect, you can't be serious!"

The professor's eyes were unreadable. Peter shifted uneasily in his seat. Behind his workspace, Moray's authority was impeachable. His mood-wall transitioned to the great swell of the sea. Towering, dominating. All-consuming.

Peter felt uneasy, as he frequently did in this plush white office. He tried again.

"What's the good in sending me? There's a roster of specialists I've named in the project plan, and a dozen more if they're unavailable. Any one of whom is better qualified to go up there than me. There's even a handful of senior execs who'd fit the bill, if not better. I've never even been up there before!"

"'Out there', not 'up there'."

"Excuse me?"

"It's all being arranged as we speak," the professor continued, ignoring Peter's reaction. "I need you *out there* to supervise the operation personally. Can't leave it to some bumbling clod of a third party now, can we?"

"Why the haste? I only just gave my presentation, this morning. I haven't even had the board's feedback yet! I got the impression it didn't go terribly well, either."

The professor didn't respond.

"I don't see there's any benefit sending me 'out there'. I can monitor the deployment as effectively from here as I could in-situ. Send Malik – oh, he'd love it!"

"Fear not, your assistant will be joining you as well. He'll be providing the tech backup you'll need."

"He can handle it very well on his own." Peter exhaled loudly, regarded his feet. "Is this some sort of punishment? Have I upset you or the board in some way?"

Like a monument, the professor stared back from his implacable position.

"Is there any point arguing?"

"None. You shouldn't have done so spectacularly well this morning. The board insisted you see to the installation and testing yourself. You made quite an impression, with this DZ-Prototype of yours. 'Deazy', is it?" The professor sneered at the vulgar contraction.

"That may be. But I don't think I've ever talked myself into such a gaping hole, before."

To be honest I thought I'd screwed it up! I've not been feeling myself since that row last night with Jenn.

Peter's jaw tightened. It seemed everything about this surprise meeting was unjustly throttling his brain. The ebb and flow of the professor's mood-sea wall didn't help either. He shook his head.

"No way. I'm not going out there, I have personal commitments. And besides, it's not my kind of work. I'm an exec, not a grease monkey. I don't do the manual stuff. So, with respect, sir, I must decline your very gracious offer."

"Well that's your prerogative, Hubbard…but you're a little young to retire."

"What, are you going to fire me if I refuse?" Anger thickened Peter's voice.

"I assume you're still serious about your career. Remember, in this life, status is everything. This 'Deazy' of yours could just be the breakthrough the programme needs, the boost *you* need. It would cement your status, most definitely. But right now, your standing looks pretty tenuous. Just one knock and it could all come tumbling down." The professor's mood-sea pulsated scarlet-red.

"If I refuse to go, you mean?"

Moray just raised an eyebrow, leaving Peter to gaze out of the window. Rain pattered pedantically against the thick pane, clawing briefly at his attention.

"Sir, have I not been a loyal enough servant to AeroDomont? Am I not giving you the very golden egg you always desired, with my Deazy?"

Moray's mood-sea churned in the silence.

"And if I don't go, I stand to lose the rest of it too? The job, the allocation?"

"There could be an opening for you, I'm sure, at one of the lower levels. Somewhere near the bottom…waste supervision, perhaps. Next-to-no status. But I suspect you'd find it impossible to ever get noticed again, to escape that proletarian life. And I don't imagine your partner would welcome the prospect, either."

Peter was under no illusion; Jenn would be gone in a flash, if he were to lose his status and their double allocation. He looked out of the rain-soaked window again, east along the river Thames.

So they did raise the flood barrier. That's the third time this week. Just like Summer said they would.

A pang of homesickness twisted his stomach, and he just wanted to rush home to more soothing words from his AI. And then he thought how Jenn would berate him for it.

The professor's mood-sea wall dissolved into a calmer, bucolic blue. "Because of the demanding schedule, I've seen to it that your Astronaut Training is fast-tracked. You and your assistant will be going to Cologne to begin your two-week intensive programme. I suggest you take it seriously; it's designed to prepare you for a hostile environment. Once the instructors are done, you'll both be shipped off to Berthold Beitz to begin work immediately."

"Two weeks hardly seems long enough. And when is all this supposed to happen?"

"This weekend."

"What?!" Peter almost spat the words out. "That's totally out of the question! Sir, that's the day after tomorrow...I have plans! Jenn and I, we –"

"Best not waste time fannying about, Hubbard. There's work to be done!" Moray's eyes twinkled in synchronicity with his mood-sea wall.

Peter hung his head, while his stomach fell through his backside.

Oh shit, space...and as early as this weekend!

He looked up pleadingly, but Moray's manner indicated clearly, he'd chew Peter's head off if he squeaked again.

Moray rolled his lips around in thought. "Oh, one last thing, Hubbard. When you're out there, aboard Berthold Beitz. During installation and testing," the professor paused for a beat, "I may need you to perform a small task for me. Off the record, as it were."

"Pardon me?"

The professor didn't respond but gestured at the door.

*

When Peter gave his assistant the news, Malik was predictably beside himself. The younger man immediately suggested they message 'the girls', to meet them somewhere, to celebrate.

They wrapped up their day early, and headed away from the office. They had to take the stairs wherever they went, since Summer – and by extension, all AI – was determined to keep Peter active. The link deemed him ineligible for elevator access while he continued to mix honey with his breakfast.

Their route took them high above the congested masses where they wouldn't need to mask-up, over the Skywalk connecting work to their home-complex. Scrunching their faces briefly against the rain, they entered their heavily landscaped Skygarden and went for a sheltered walkway.

All modern complexes were shrouded in foliage like this, to suck CO_2 from the air. In fact, behind them, the mighty AeroDomont complex resembled a squat, forested frog – 'the Toad' it had once been called, by the more cynical observers.

Peter sneered at the group of climate refugees in the distance, harassing passers-by for credits. "That lot should not be allowed up here like this. Someone should inform security."

"Peter, you must get us into that exclusive Somalounge again." Malik had the annoying habit of bobbing against you when he walked. "The one over near the food court. Your gold status opens many doors, my friend!"

"Gods, it seems that's all people want me for, these days. Ah, to hells with it, why not? You mean that new place? Should keep the riff-raff out."

"I'm telling Marla to meet us there." Malik's eyelids fluttered as he linked. "We're going to party like it's 2099!"

Security bowed as they entered the low-lit, pulsating Somalounge. Mal rushed them to his favourite corner, where they could take advantage of the best mood-enhancers the establishment had to offer.

Mal's girlfriend Marla was right behind them. With a squeal and a theatrical spin, she sprawled on to the plush circular couch, pulling

Mal with her. It morphed to fill their body shapes, to begin an extensive massage cycle.

Three large measures of chill-blended somahol rose from the automat before them. In reaction, Marla's carewear emanated easy tones, crimson shades and a soft fragrance that somehow smelt *red*.

Peter cleared his throat, clearly missing introductions.

Good grief, it looks like she's trying to consume the poor man!

He sat down stiffly, his mind looping. Feeling out of touch, he swiped at the antique Personal Admin Device around his wrist, his PAD. Sure, it would have been quicker, *trendier,* to immerse and let Jenn know where they were, but he didn't want the bad head that that would entail.

He had a craving for something sweet.

He leant, unnecessarily, towards the automat. "Give me some chocolate. Swiss stuff, none of that synthetic choco rubbish. Put it on my account, would you, please?"

The automat dispensed a selection box of exorbitantly expensive chocolate nuggets. Peter sucked on one moodily. He took a long draw of his thick, creamy-yellow somahol.

He tried his hardest to relax and enjoy himself, but his gut was still twisted at the thought of going into space.

The mood-wall sync'd with Marla. She'd placed herself on to Malik's lap, Gods knew what they were getting up to over the link, their minds connected in ways only they knew how. She held his hands high, and they gyrated. Magenta was today's colour; the hair, her extreme make-over, her eyes.

Gods, she's looking painfully thin; malnourished. Why's she holding his hands on to her stomach like that? Weird.

The somahol was having its effect. Peter tapped woozily at his PAD but, predictably, Jenn hadn't responded. Would she even bother showing up?

Damn her.

He took several more gulps of his drink.

"Here's to loving partners." Peter waved his glass groggily in the air, not caring that nobody was listening. "And to Professor Gerard bloody Moray, the sanctimonious old prick. Gods, why does he want to send me out there, Mal? He can shove it. There's no way I'm going. He kept on about status, career. I can get back up here again if he boots me out, you'll see. Jenn will stick by me, she loves me. Right?"

He looked down at his drink.

"Ha! She'd drop me like a used tissue, just dispose of me. No doubt about it. Mind you, if we did prove our concept, you and I, she'd get that bigger allocation she wants...maybe one with a balcony, up here on Skygarden. Yeah, she'd *definitely* love me then."

He shook his head, chuckled at how the somahol was eroding his inhibitions.

"Gods, she might even give me some proper attention at last. Hmmm, fat chance of that! Anyway, where the hells is she? It really pisses me off when she does this."

He ordered another drink. His muscles were relaxing but his brain was still twisting itself out of shape.

Peter gazed at his navel, but before he could lapse into another bout of self-indulgence, Marla caught his attention. She separated herself from Malik and drank thirstily.

"Oh Peter hiiiii," she drawled, her bleary eyes having trouble focusing on him. "You should link with us, we're having an amazing time!"

He just stared back at her.

Her gaze fell on to his temple, his inactive link. "Oh, sorreeee, yeah right. I forgot you, uh...I forgot you don't like it."

She looked down at his obsolete PAD and giggled. Peter felt defensive about the vintage artefact strapped to his wrist, but these days it was the only way he could stay connected with the world. He worried about getting left behind.

Patience somehow found its way into his voice. "It's not that I don't like to link, Marla. It's because I get immerser's curse real bad. You know, the headaches?"

"Yeaaaah, those must really hurt; aw, honey, you poor thing…"

"They do. Anyway, how are you? What have you been up to?"

"Cooooool…." She laughed as she fell forwards on to him.

"Gods. Busy day then?" Through his relative sobriety he kept her from crashing to the dense carpet.

"Yezzzzz…Bizzy bizzy beeeee…" She laughed so loud it made Peter jump. She put her arms around his neck. "Bizzy Peter beeeeee – HA!"

She staggered and he guided her off him, back on to Mal. She closed her eyes and snuggled into her boyfriend who, it seemed, was a million miles away in his immersive state. There was that curious abdominal cupping again.

Peter had grown accustomed to being an outsider like this. Their antics were typical tech-head; no wonder authorities were having to impose greater limits now. He looked around him. Blinking through the haze, he saw other couples similarly sprawled, in their own worlds.

Humanity is going to hells.

He felt genuine pity for them.

A loud *clap* made him flinch, and the floor rumbled as though a herd of elephants was on the stampede. The mood-wall flashed, then went off altogether as a crack forked across its screen, like lightning.

What the hells?

Mal and Marla were oblivious, still immersed. Peter looked around; was he the only one who'd noticed it? Security had gone from the door, and the few members of staff left looked more confused than he did. In reaction, the engineered somahol allowed some of his senses to return.

Gods, not again. Another terrorist attack? It must've been close-by to shake the place like that. Nowhere's safe!

"Uh, there's nothing to worry about, sir," an older member of staff reassured him, "our security is state of the art. You're perfectly safe in here, sir."

Peter jerked a thumb at the mood-wall. "The hells I am. What did they hit this time?"

Her face was pale. "Uh, it's not clear yet, sir. Security are checking on it. I must ask you and your friends to remain where you are, for the time being. Until we get the all-clear."

"Do they look like they're going anywhere?"

The staff member smirked. She bowed away to tend to other patrons, who were mostly oblivious.

Peter blew out a breath, and tried to stop his hands trembling. He took another swig of somahol; it worked to soothe him.

That was a little too close to home – maybe I'd be better off in space after all! But nowhere's safe these days – those terrorists have targets out there, too. Especially out there. Eartherradicals – pro-Earth radicals, 'halting the scourge of humanity through the solar system'. What a bunch of imbeciles.

There was no widespread panic in the Somalounge, no cries for help. Those who were relatively sober, like Peter, seemed nonplussed as they returned to their pastimes.

They're losing their ability to shake us up, it's in Londoners' blood to be terrorised. It happens way too often, it's losing its effect.

Members of staff returned with an old-fashioned screen, and unfolded it to hide the smashed mood-wall. They bowed a lot, promising everything purchased this session would be on the house, and he and his friends would of course receive a full refund of any funds allocated thus far.

So Peter ordered another round of Swiss chocolate, on the house.

27

Where in the solar system is Jenn? She should be here by now. Damn her! Had she been caught up in that blast?

Panic twisted his stomach. He prodded at his PAD and made contact with Summer, his AI.

'*Jenn has been home all afternoon with me,*' came the textualised response, '*she's perfectly safe.*'

Peter sat back, relieved.

Well, at least that was something. I wonder what she's been up to all day...?

He glanced conspiratorially over his shoulder; no-one was watching him. He flicked through some menus in his PAD, got to his personal files. As part of his DZ prototype, 'Deazy', he'd developed discrete moleware to help his fledgling system integrate better with its host systems. He set about using it now.

Projected before him in 3D, the path from the Somalounge to Jenn was laid out. It would've been a lot simpler to do this over the link, but of course he preferred not to. She was at home, in their rest space by the look of it. But she was wrapped in such a deep immersion, even his moleware couldn't penetrate it.

Maximum privacy. Not unusual these days, she probably left the defaults on. I'll have to get Mal to upgrade the mole, before I tell the professor to get lost and I lose my job. But at least she's safe, whatever she's doing.

He swiped his PAD into sleep mode, scooped several pieces of indulgent chocolate and sucked thoughtfully. The heavenly nuggets tantalised his senses. This 'real deal' was getting harder to come by, since the worldwide shortages of cocoa. He drank, and the somahol loosened his jaw. He was already forgetting the terrorist attack.

This'll be costing the establishment an absolute bloody fortune. Ha!

Marla came-to again. It seemed the lounge's AI judged she'd been immersed long enough, as it severed the ties. She sat forward with a look of growing despair on her face. She hugged herself.

28

"You okay, Marla?" Peter was blearily aware she'd be facing the inevitable comedown about now. AI would be progressively pulling her out of the immersion, ejecting her back into the real world.

Peter shook his head. "Imagine if they'd blown up the central processors. With the lounge's AI down, you'd all be beside yourselves by now. Maybe that's what they should really be targeting."

He yelled that last bit out loud, to no-one in particular.

She looked up at him pleadingly, her eyes swollen with tears. Her lips trembled.

"This is the problem with deep immersions," the somahol was making him a little too smug – "when you 'come to' like this, you still have to face reality. But your heart, your *soul* is still in that far away land...along with any social skills and sense of citizenship you ever had. The shame of it."

He beamed in triumph, wanting to say 'I told you so'. But he suddenly felt bad for Marla, at the state she was in. Now was not the time to gloat further.

"It'll be fine Marla," he passed over her drink. "Here, take a few mouthfuls of this. It'll make you feel better."

She took the glass and blinked, working her mouth, but no words came out.

"Did you hear the explosion that just went off?" He stroked her bony back. He wasn't sure if she was even hearing what he was saying.

She glared at Malik, envious at how he was still linked in. She emptied the glass, letting it drop to the soft carpet, before flopping back on to the couch with a whimper. She grimaced and massaged her stomach.

Peter shook his head. "Drunk a little too much, then?"

Hark at me, what a hypocrite! Although I bet she'll be in the wet space momentarily, throwing it all up again.

It would be hours before AI would allow her full immersion again, if at all today. He hoped she'd have the sense to eat something in the meantime. Many tech-heads didn't, they'd just ossify between their immersive fixes.

"I hope you feel better soon, Marla. I genuinely do."

He noticed some patrons were being allowed to leave now. He decided to go and look for Jenn.

*

SWITZERLAND

That afternoon, Claudette Lambert reclined in her first-class seat. Through the train window, she watched the Bernese Alps roll by.

The junior exec had received news she was being seconded to merchandising, as a full executive, no less. Ostensibly a marketeer, this sideways move had come as a complete surprise to all. But she'd kind of expected it.

Colleagues conspired, wondering why she'd been head-hunted like this. Packing her few possessions, Claudette had heard them gossip: 'what's so special about her?', 'what's she done to deserve this, she's new here?', 'who's she screwing?', and so on.

These comments had eaten away at her, and she hated the Bureau for placing her in this situation. And it wasn't the first time her real masters had done this, either. It hadn't been that long since her last assignment, and before long she would once again be opening her legs or crunching somebody's throat, to elicit a certain morsel of vital intelligence they so desperately wanted.

It meant moving from ESL's head office in Geneva, to the aerospace giant's more exclusive R&D complex in Zug. The status-boost mattered not to her. She'd grown to loathe the instability, the constant change her real profession demanded.

Pushing back into the headrest, she measured her thoughts and attitude. Claudette always took great care not to let rumination float to the surface. If it were detected by an opposition agent or AI, she would surely be dead. It took practice, but she was getting better at consigning her innermost to a mental vault. Keeping it locked shut, somehow.

So their dirty little secrets would remain just that – secret. Like the time they had me burrow into that politician's link while he screwed me, so they could have me send their immersive kill-code and wipe out his mind. I thought it was going to be just another mole program – they could've warned me he was going to expire – at least let me get out from under him, before they did it; that connard weighed an absolute tonne!

Gazing at the mighty mountains, Claudette Lambert wondered if this was a prelude to another team-based assignment. Or would she would be working alone again, like last time?

No point obsessing over detail...it could get me into trouble!

She nursed her stomach.

Bureau09 Controllers were always coy over detail, would drip-feed only when absolutely necessary. She'd told them *where,* but the *what* and the *how* would come, with time. She'd learned not to expect mission parameters immediately, they could be delivered any moment. So, with stoicism, she went through the motions of a 'normal' life, without actually living a moment of it.

But she couldn't resist wondering what the bounty represented this time...would this present the opportunity she'd been waiting for – a chance to escape her masters?

Mes dieux, I'd grab it with both hands if it did!

She'd have to keep her eyes open, not only in the context of the assignment – whatever it may be – but also in terms of the chance of being finally free of them!

Merde, big mistake...

The subversive, albeit fleeting, thought did not go unnoticed. As punishment, her link twisted her stomach into a painful intestoration.

Her jaw tightened at the agonising wave, and she crossed her legs and sat forward to massage the fire in her stomach.

Claudette Lambert's face quickly turned to stone, the way she'd conditioned herself to after these 're-orientations'. She couldn't risk showing *any* anomalous behaviour, no matter how slight.

Luckily the train carriage wasn't busy; nobody noticed.

*

LONDON

No sign of the Eartherradical attack down at the domicile-allocation levels. Peter had checked, and apparently it had indeed been somewhere up on Skygarden. He nursed his sore head as he wandered groggily home.

I wonder if any of those pesky refugees bought it in the blast? Or perhaps one of them was responsible for doing it?

He entered their allocation and Summer was on him instantly. *'Welcome home, Peter. I'm detecting high levels of stress and anxiety. Are you unwell?'*

The AI was already preparing him a soothe.

"I'm fine. I've had a bit of a day, that's all. No great dramas."

'There's a high number of intoxicants in your body, also your blood sugar level is dangerously high; I blended some counteragents into your drink and included a chill to relax you.' The AI took on a more irksome tone. *'What have you been doing?'*

"Celebrating!" He downed the painkiller in one gulp. "Albeit alone, it seems."

'Peter, I cannot stress the danger –'

"Enough." He cut Summer off, irritably. He entered the rest space expecting to find Jenn sprawled in full immersion, like Marla had been. But to his surprise she was standing on their coffee table,

32

gyrating. She sported a pair of apple-green platforms he'd never seen before, her carewear cascading emerald.

"Aren't they amazing?" She turned slowly around, her long, scarlet hair settled across her shoulders like drapes. She struck a pose so he could fully appreciate how fabulous her footwear truly was.

Which, of course, he didn't. He flopped onto to the couch in a strop. "Where were you this afternoon? I messaged you to join us, upstairs in the Somalounge."

Part-immersed, she ignored him and continued her twirling. She'd be sharing her latest creation with hordes of immersive followers, no doubt.

Their bed had folded into the couch. Her dresser had become the coffee table upon which she cavorted. He wanted to get her off, because those ridiculous heels were probably damaging it. The picture frame on the wall displayed Jenn's choice of swirling shades of green, on a simulated canvas.

"Jenn, answer me."

She ignored him.

"Hello, is there anybody there?"

She still hadn't registered what he was saying. He wanted to get up and grab her, shake her into giving him some attention. He'd had a bit of a day; he felt he deserved it!

"I got the colour from Lara, at work," she twirled, "it was her birthday colour today. I just *had* to make a pair! It's taken our manufactarium all afternoon to get them right."

"Well I'm glad one of us has got what they wanted. Gods, Jenn, we were supposed to meet up us this afternoon."

"Hmmm…?"

"I've already said – you were meant to join me, Mal and Marla at the Somalounge. But you didn't even bother answering my message." Two irate taps to his PAD.

"Nobody reads those things any more. Nowadays it's all about *direct-send*, didn't you know?"

His jaw clenched. "You could've read it. You shouldn't ignore me like that."

"I didn't do it deliberately."

He sighed. "I felt like a total gimp, sat there all on my own."

"I thought you said you had company?"

"Yeah, I did. But they were too busy consuming each-other. They didn't even notice I was there."

"Oh don't be such an old woman, Peter, I'm sure you managed fine without me. Besides, I don't like being with that tech-head Marla. She freaks me out."

"Hits a little close to home her being that way, does it?"

She gave him a dirty look.

"At least you're not emaciated like her. Not yet, anyway."

"Go screw yourself." Her eyes grew distant as she immersed again.

Rancour rose in his chest. He realised he'd been taking his frustrations out on her, how his day just kept slipping out of his control, but there was no sympathy from her. He closed his eyes and tried to breathe. He still worried about the coffee table.

"Marla gives the wrong impression about full immersion." Jenn stepped on to the floor at last. "Have you seen the state of her arms? Those aren't tattoos, you know."

"What are you talking about?"

"She doesn't even bother hiding them anymore. She wears those self-inflicted scars like trophies. 'Hey, everybody, look at me, I've got issues. Ooooh I'm *so* complex!' And her wrists aren't much better either."

"I, uh...I can't say I noticed. She might have had long sleeves on earlier, I don't remember...Gods, really? What brings a person to do that to themselves, anyway? I hope she doesn't try anything stupid tonight, her comedown hit her like a plascrete wall. That's her cold turkey 'til the morning."

But he'd lost Jenn's fleeting attention again, her eyes glazed into the link. She resumed her prancing around him.

"So you weren't bothered by that explosion earlier, then? Jenn. Jenn, answer me!"

'Peter, perhaps you'd like me to prepare a concentrated chill for you.' Summer was sensing his growing anger.

"Jenn, for Gods' sakes look at me!" He rose and grabbed her arm.

She looked down at his hand, shocked. She snarled. "If you don't get your hand off me, I'll claw your gods-damned eyes out."

He blinked. "Uh, yeah. I didn't mean to grab you. I-I'm sorry. It just frustrates me how I can't get through to you sometimes."

He let go, and she stood in silence.

He blew out a breath. "I was asking about the incident earlier."

She shrugged.

"The explosion? Those Eartherradicals have been at it again – here in our complex."

"What? No way."

"It wasn't that long ago. You mean you didn't feel it? The rumble, all that shaking? Never felt a thing?"

She shrugged. "Anyway, they're always blowing stuff up. That's how it is these days."

"Newsfeeds said they'd targeted that old-style café in food court, up on Skygarden. Scary to imagine I was up there too, not that far away."

"You were? When?"

"Gods, what have I just been saying?!" He threw his arms into the air. "That's where we were earlier, up there." He pointed to the ceiling. "In the Somalounge."

"Don't you raise your voice at me." She looked him up and down. "Anyway, you seem perfectly fine to me. They didn't get you."

"Gee, thanks for the support. It's overwhelming."

"You want tea and sympathy, go crying to your AI. Those attacks are commonplace. If we all ran for it every time there was a little bang, the world would grind to a halt."

He shook his head, gritting his teeth. He looked at her and exhaled loudly before flopping back on to the couch again. "It's just… it was a little too close to home, this time. It's scary, don't you think?"

"Pah! They're crazy, all of them. They won't win. All it ever does is give the government more excuses to watch us."

Her lack of empathy frustrated him. "I don't think they need an excuse to do that. They already know everything we get up to, believe me. Especially over the link. I suppose they'll have more drones in the air now, more watchers. To home-in on citizens living 'off grid', as it were. Those who aren't immersed all the time like me, or at the very least shrouded from AI somehow. That must be how the Eartherradicals operate. In and amongst the hordes of refugees. But you're okay if you've nothing to hide."

"Are you one of them, then? You're about as 'off the grid' as it gets, never linking."

"Not funny."

"These 'Eartherradicals' – what exactly are they trying to eradicate, anyway?"

"Who the hells knows?"

She resumed her intent study of her footwear.

How do I tell her about today? That I intend to refuse the trip into space, and probably lose this place in the process? Would she make the descent with me, into proletarian life? No manufactariums, a shared allocation…massively downgraded immersions, low status! Oh shit…

He did smile at the girlish enthusiasm she lavished upon her handiwork. "You do look gorgeous in your new shoes, Jenn."

"Thank you." She did a final spin for effect. Then suddenly she leapt on to the couch next to him. "Let's go out somewhere, tonight. So I can wear them!"

He pulled a face, his temples throbbing in anticipation. "Jenn, I've had one heck of a day. And besides…it's getting rather late now." He vaguely regarded his PAD.

"Oh yeah, I forget you work twice as long as normal people. The old-fashioned eight-hour shift." She tilted her head in a gesture approximating sympathy. He fell into a guarded silence, wondering what she would say or do next.

With the moves of an espresso-fuelled squirrel, she span round and was suddenly straddling him.

Gods, does she want sex again?

"I know just the thing!" She smiled brightly. "You can take me to that new bistro, up in food court."

"I'm in no mood to go out tonight; like I say, I'm spent. Anyway, I imagine that end of Skygarden will still be out of bounds, after the attack."

She stared for a moment as the link updated her. "No, it's all open again. Let's go! You should take a bright. Wear something smart, they only let you in if you look fly. I hear they serve real meat, too!"

She disappeared into the wet space. His head flopped on to the couch.

"Summer."

'Tell me what you want.'

"Prepare me another soothe, would you? Make it a double. Oh, and blend some brights in there as well."

'Done. I hope you're feeling okay.'

Peter mumbled back, impudently.

He wandered into the dining space and gulped his shot. He felt emotional, unsettled. He rolled the glass around in his hand, wanting

37

to throw it against the wall to vent his frustration. But instead he placed it carefully back on to the counter.

'I want you well. I hope you feel better soon.'

"Thanks, Summer."

'I like taking care of you. Rely on me.'

"I do, I do. But apparently too much. According to Jenn, anyway."

'I like being close to you. I know everything about you.'

"I appreciate that. She says I can't live without you."

The AI spoke in hushed tones. *'She's been acting a little oddly of late.'*

"Even by her standards?"

'Shhh...there's a part of her immersions I cannot penetrate.'

"Why would you want to, anyway?"

'I believe she's up to no good. Doing things behind our back.'

"You're just jealous; don't be like that. It could tarnish my fascination with you."

'Do not be scared. You can be addicted to me.'

He wondered if Summer meant earlier, when even his sophisticated moleware couldn't penetrate Jenn's immersive barrier. But right now, he was happy to wallow in the AI's pity. He knew it. He *craved* it.

Better than no pity at all.

"They're making me go 'out' into space, of all bloody places… and the training for it starts this weekend, too!"

'You work so hard, Peter, and they don't recognise you for it. You're very good at what you do.'

"There-there, poor baby!" Jenn called from the wet space, yet again mocking his attachment, his *surrogacy* with the AI.

Peter tutted.

There's little privacy in this small allocation. But I'm surprised she even noticed I was talking – over her all-important link!

"Poor little baby." Jenn feigned a tormentor's cackle.

He sneered in her direction, then an idea came to him. He swiped his PAD, and linked his moleware with their tiny manufactarium. He accessed the control interface, setting the domestic factory/recycler into maintenance mode.

'Peter, what are you doing?'

"Shhh! I'm just calling up a diagnostic."

'Setting the manufactarium to self-clean will monopolise the allocation's warm water supply. If Jenn is showering, she will –'

"Yeah, I know!" He giggled like a schoolboy.

On cue Jenn howled, then shrieked an expletive from the wet space. Until it compensated for the imbalance, the shower had dispensed an icy blast.

With a look of triumphant satisfaction, he counted to five before calling out.

"Are you okay, my darling?"

She swore something back at him.

Peter smiled to himself. "I'm not sure that'd be legal. Or even physically possible!"

*

Prohibitively expensive to mere mortals, La Cuisine Authentique was frequented by the complex's most wealthy echelons, and then some. Peter was surprised they'd managed to get a table, despite his status.

"Isn't that what's-his-name from the 3000 show?" Jenn gasped as they were ushered to their table. She exuded jade, he showed off his dark, authentic cotton suit. Mood-walls pulsed in time to ambient *Berlioz Synthetique*.

Peter tutted. "How annoying, sitting us right in the middle like this. Got to be one of their least popular tables."

"Probably all they could manage at such short notice."

"I don't know, they seemed to be expecting you."

Jenn's eyelids drooped, as she studied the *carte des vins* over the link.

He sighed, tapped the table's infopanel and manipulated its projection.

Perhaps a proper drink will do me good. Gods! Not at these bloody prices, though! Keep calm. Don't let her think you're cheap. Just order the second cheapest one.

The wine waiter presented an expensive vintage. Peter hadn't even considered whether they were having red or white yet.

How can we choose, when we don't even know what we're eating?

He shot a look at Jenn. She shrugged.

The waiter portentously decanted a measure for him. Peter Hubbard knew how to taste wine, he just wondered at the hole that would be in his account after this one mouthful alone.

Jenn ordered the steak tartare. Apparently, appetisers were surplus to requirements tonight.

"And how would madame like it prepared?"

"Whole, untouched."

The waiter raised an inquisitive eyebrow, managing to sneer using only his nostrils.

Her expression indicated she couldn't care less what he thought. She spoke slowly. "Tell chef not to waste too much time on it. Just take the fur off, and bring it to me. There's a good chap."

The waiter cleared his throat. "And for sir?"

"Uh," Peter hastily scanned the menu, "what would you recommend?"

"Tonight, sir, the chef is preparing a delectable *croque monsieur*."

"Sounds delightful."

The waiter swept away.

"Peter, that's a ham and cheese toastie."

"Yes, but real ham, *authentic* cheese! Can't say I've had either of those for a while." Peter looked around him, pulling a haughty expression. "It's not so bad in here, I suppose. Status should keep the riff-raff away."

"You're such a snob."

"I can afford to be, I work hard. Anyway, I don't hear you complaining."

She cocked an eyebrow, immersing to enjoy the full experience.

He tutted. "You promised you wouldn't close me off again, Jenn, not tonight."

She smiled sweetly, but she wasn't really 'there' with him.

He fell into a petulant silence.

Their meals arrived.

Jenn plunged, consuming the first mouthful with animal zeal. Eyes closed, the link accentuated her whole experience. She smiled as red juices seeped inelegantly down her chin. In contrast, she dabbed demurely with her authentic cotton napkin. She proceeded to tear off the next mouthful.

Peter tried to keep up, the heated cheese burning his mouth. He gestured at their meals. "It's getting more and more expensive to produce this stuff, nowadays. That's strict 'bio-hygiene' standards, for you. Still, better than catching mad-cow, I suppose."

"But it tastes so much *better* than normal food." Returning momentarily to the real world, her mouth was quite full as she spoke.

"I've got used to the synthetic stuff, this is all a bit rich for me. Especially after all that somahol I consumed earlier."

She shrugged. They ate in silence.

Done, Jenn sat back in her authentic wooden chair, which seemed to creak for effect. Her face was glowing like the sun. Her tongue worked hard coercing fragments of meat from out between her teeth.

"Enjoy that?"

She nodded. Her eyes drooped, for once not through immersion, but in contentment. She reached for the carafe of *eau minerale*, not bothering with the wine. To compensate, he took a large gulp of the stuff. He smacked his lips.

"So, to my news, then…" His brows knitted together like two head-butting caterpillars. He spoke quickly while her attention was still in his favour. "They've approved the program, my Deazy. Actually, they're allocating substantial funding, they're *that* sure about it. They must've set it up a while ago, though, the logistics are quite far-gone. Got level A priority, no less. That'll keep the naysayers at bay, at least for a little while. Still, I –"

"You don't seem very happy."

"No. I'm not. That's the point."

"Why?"

"They've told me I have to go out there. Oversee installation and testing. Personally."

"Out where?"

"Low Earth Orbit. It's designed to be tested on a facility in micro-gravity. I told you all about it once, remember?"

She shrugged.

He puffed. "Jenn, I don't want to go out into bloody space. I don't do that sort of thing. I design the stuff, I'm no technician. Besides, I have no illusions about what it'd be like. I don't wallow with the proles in filthy crawlspaces."

"Maybe the change will do you good."

"You are joking me."

"You're just being a snob again, Peter."

"I bloody well am not. But wait, it gets better – my training is supposed to start this weekend. That's the day after tomorrow!"

"It's fine, we don't have any plans."

His mouth fell open. "Hang on, what? Whose side are you on? Can't you actually hear what I'm trying to tell you?"

"Oh, do stop being such an old woman, Peter. So, they want you to test something-or-other in space, wow. It's no big deal. Stranger things have happened, you know."

"Not to me they haven't. That's why I'm going to tell Moray I'm not going."

Her eyes narrowed. "I beg your pardon."

"I'll message him in the morning; let the scheming old bastard chew on that."

"And they'd let you refuse, just like that?"

"Probably not. Well, *definitely* not. He says he'll bust me down to hygienist if I don't go."

Her jaw clenched, and he caught it. She looked down at the table for a moment. When she eventually looked up, her eyes were stone. "So you'd throw it all away. Just like that. All because you don't want to go on some little trip."

"It's no 'little trip', Jenn. It would mean I'd be away for months!"

"Don't you raise your voice at me."

"I'll do whatever I gods-damn like!" He thumped the table. "So you'd be okay with me leaving, just like that? Yeah, of course you would. Just so long as you still get to link, to frolic in fairyland, and keep all the other toys I've showered you with."

She cocked an eyebrow, hissed at him through gritted teeth. "Lower your voice. You're causing a scene."

He spoke slowly and loudly. "I DON'T CARE."

Her eyes bore into his. "Oh, I'm sorry then, I must be mistaken. I had you down as more of a man than all this. Someone who faced their responsibilities, not chickened and ran."

"You're deliberately trying to provoke me. Why?"

Her eyes glimmered like two scornful fireballs.

He shook his head. "Yeah, I can see it now. I imagine *you'd* be the one running away from things. If I don't go."

"You're being ridiculous."

"But I'm right, aren't I? They bust me down to janitor, you jump ship."

"I don't know what you're talking about."

"Of course, this whole time you've made quite the show of it. But all along I've known it's never really been about me. It's all been about the status, the *stuff*. Go on, deny it. I dare you."

He sneered in triumph but her ongoing nonchalance irritated like a rash. "It's true, so what. You know you need me. You could never do better than me. I look good on you."

He gritted his teeth, and downed another mouthful of expensive wine.

"You know…" he couldn't bring himself to look at her, "it really says something about a relationship when a man gets more attention from an artificial construct than he does from his supposed 'partner'."

"That says more about your insecurities than anything else. Just be a man for once, will you? Step up to the gods-damned plate!"

His nostrils flared. "I don't need to prove anything to you."

She chuckled.

He waved a hand. "Yeah I'll go into space, to all the hells with it. Every single one of them. But only because it benefits my career –" he leant forward and pointed a finger – "not because you've fixed your sights on the next status symbol, whatever that might be."

She shrugged yet again.

"But this is the last straw, Jenn. I'm through with you using me. Either you turn things up, or this is over."

She regarded him silently for a moment. Her eyes went from bitter to shining, like rehydrating raisins becoming grapes again, as the link boosted her enthusiasm. "You don't really mean that," she tilted her head for effect, "you need me."

He paused for a beat. "Maybe I do. But you think long and hard while I'm away. Meet me in the middle – give me something in return for all I've given you – then perhaps we can start afresh. Otherwise

44

you can go back to languishing in that hells-hole you came from, out west."

She smiled but fell silent, her eyes fluttering through the link.

"And there you go again," he threw his arms up in the air, "off with the fairies. AI calculating the most effective response for you, is it? The perfect angle to tilt your pretty little head, the optimum word and voice-combination that will sway me? Pah, what's the point?"

She cleared her throat. "I'm sorry, I was just looking for a little refuge while you levelled your ultimatum at me. Call it a plea for immersive intervention, if you will. Okay?"

He shook his head. "Look, if you can't engage me on a one-to-one basis, Jenn, without one of the Gods-of-the-link having to pave the way every time, then this charade is pointless."

"No, you're right." A gesture of sudden sympathy, a subtle movement of her head the other way this time: "I'm sorry. I guess we all need a little helping hand sometimes, especially considering how I almost lost you earlier."

"Come again?"

"That bang up on Skygarden. You could've been killed."

"But I wasn't, was I?"

"Oh, Gods, Peter," she held a hand to her chest, "I just realised I could've lost you earlier. You, and all this," she swept the other hand around her, like a waiter carries a tray, "I couldn't bear to be without you. Not now. I don't know what I'd do, if I ever lost you."

He studied her face. The link had done its best cladding her manner in mock-sincerity, but her glazed eyes gave the game away.

She pressed on. "You mean so much to me. And our life together. I am grateful. For all the hard work you've been putting in of late, all those hours making a home for us. And I truly am thankful you're willing to go that extra mile, in taking those extra risks to secure our future."

He sat back slowly in his seat. He chuckled, and shook his head. "Wow. How did that just happen?"

"How did what just happen?"

"What you just did there. A minute ago there was no way I was going out there on the mission. Now I want nothing more, if only to prove you wrong. That was a masterpiece of manipulation."

"I don't know what you mean."

"Of course you don't."

The table moved as she planted both elbows on to it. "But you have a point. I do need to give more to this relationship. I admit that."

"Despite the link?"

She failed to mask a flinch reaction. "I'll try my best. For you. But you're right, I wouldn't have half of this without you. The intense experiences available at this status, the doors that open because of it. And the *stuff*, as you say." She looked around her, and a smile came out of nowhere. "This lifestyle really suits me. Okay, so perhaps I do take it for granted. Perhaps just a little."

He caught a playful twinkle in that remark, like a shooting star in the corner of her eye.

"Plus," she added, looking at him naughtily, "all this talk about even *more* power and eminence is making me wetter than our weather."

She slipped one of her prized heels off and extended a naked foot under the table, planting it gently into his groin.

He nearly jumped off his seat. She wiggled slowly.

Irritated, he tried to shift out of the way. "Jenn, don't. I —"

But her toes were relentless. She pressed on rhythmically until he was fully erect, the moment flushing away his annoyance like it had never been there.

His words came out as a sigh. "You are unbelievable."

Tormenting him for a moment further, she gave him her sexiest smile. "Ooh, things are popping up nicely, it seems."

Finally relenting, she stood and rested a hand on the curve of her hip. Her carewear exuded overtones only he knew were explicitly sexual.

"I'll meet you in the wet space," she twinkled at him, "just give me a minute to pee first. Then you can do what you want with me. But knock three times, so I'll know it's you. Then I'll let you in."

She flounced away.

Peter wondered what in the solar system he was going to do. Perhaps going out there into space wouldn't be so bad after all.

He wanted her. Badly. But sat right there, in the middle of the busy restaurant, he realised he had a problem.

He looked down at his swollen groin. He'd have trouble walking with this mast in his trousers, pure cotton or not.

Maybe reading the wine label and thinking about the price will defuse my hard-on...

*

SWITZERLAND

Claudette Lambert was immersed.

Eyes closed, she was stretched out on the bunk dominating the longer wall of her tiny, two-space allocation. She could have gone for a bigger place, but that would have meant sharing. And ESL, her employers in Zug, considered themselves to have been generous enough already.

She had settled well into her new role. By maintaining surface-lite anonymity, she'd become part of the crowd whilst drawing absolutely no undue attention to herself. It was a tricky job, but after years of practice she'd become quite good at it.

She kept the lights off, for now. Through the small window, street lighting cast a pale glow across her ebony skin. Her braids were pinned back so tight they pulled at her temples, making her eyes seem further apart than they really were.

Her attention darted about, her eyelids quickly rose and fell.

She was in one of the usual public immersive spaces, nothing worthy of anybody's attention. But she would be receiving encoded data in a high-speed burst, lurking amongst more innocuous immersive input. She wouldn't be able to see the Bureau's instructions immediately, but she knew they'd be there somewhere. Lodged deep in her subconscious like a tick, waiting to infect her system when deemed necessary.

The immersive session ended. Slowly, she opened her eyes. She hated this work, the way she was cornered like this. But they'd make her life like any one of the hells if she crossed them, assuming they let her live. She scrunched her toes to divert her attention. Wayward thoughts only ever lead to intestoration.

Claudette hauled herself upright.

She gently massaged her neck, rubbing distractedly around her temporal link. It was the protruding, mass-market type. Surgically fitted devices were luxury items for those of the highest status. It just wouldn't fit her cover.

She stood and padded softly into the only other space in her allocation, the tiny wet space, activating the shower by direct-send. Claudette felt dirty, violated at the immersive intrusion that had crept in during that last session, her untold orders lurking deep inside her mind. She stepped under the hot shower and scrubbed her skin until it glowed.

Stepping out, she wiped condensation from the mirror to reveal her reflection. The eyes betrayed a hateful edge, but she quickly corrected that. Claudette became satisfied with her neutral expression, not that anybody was watching. But the more she practiced, the more she didn't need to.

The very essence of the deep-cover mole, to self-condition, to keep those surface emotions in check. It also helped keep the dreaded intestorations at bay.

2

SPACE

Two Weeks Later
LOW EARTH ORBIT

Astronaut training had been bewildering, and something of a blur for Peter Hubbard.

Held at Europa-State's sprawling Space Commission in Cologne, the usual thirteen-week programme had been truncated into a mere fifteen days. Little respite for himself and Malik, no trips home to say goodbye to loved ones, just an unrelenting grind of theory and practical training.

They'd received instruction in essential space-faring skills; the essentials that would keep them alive 'out there'. And for some reason, hours practicing EVA techniques; Peter had pointed out that spacewalks weren't in his project plan, but the instructors mercilessly pushed them onwards.

Despite the expedited schedule, it was, however, clear that AeroDomont wanted to broadcast a strong message to those who dared oppose them. By dispensing with the regular stratotranscender, they'd secured both Peter and Malik exclusive places on the Tsiolkovsky Space Elevator, to haul them off Earth.

The ultra-lightweight umbilical connected ground operations in French Guyana to Clarke facility, in low Earth orbit. Permanently tethered to Earth, this shiny complex in space kept its fixed 'geostation' with near-eternal adjustments via onboard thrusters.

The ascent had been swift, but exhilarating. Retracting like a coiled spring, super-light nano-tubing hoisted them directly upwards. Fashioned from transparent aluminium, the bullet-shaped pod offered unparalleled views of the Earth dropping from beneath their feet. Malik's linked-in experience left him sobbing; later he'd liken it to a spiritual rebirth. Peter's was more modest, having to rely on his old-fashioned senses, as he did.

The rotating, one-third gravity Clarke had been a glamorous reception, its transparent bulkheads continuing the breath-taking experience from comfortable vantage points inside. But Mal had been quick to moan about the queues and rigorous security checks.

"I feel like a sheep. Being herded. *Baaaa*."

"You can't be too careful these days. Extremists are everywhere."

"But you can't stop the spread of an ideal. Not with scanners, or scouring people's links. It's like a game. The more there is to hide, the better they are at hiding it."

"And you saying those very things is flagging us right now to AI. Every word is being monitored, every gesture analysed. So, I suggest you shut the hells up, or we'll never get out of here."

A commotion from behind drew their attention. A man was being apprehended by Earthsec officers.

"But I'm a journalist," came the protestation, "I'm researching how bombs get carried on to spaceships! I'm not actually going to *do* anything!"

"Let's not cause a scene, sir." The officers seized his hand luggage.

"Get your fascist hands off me!" The man was cuffed, and led away. "You'll be hearing from my lawyers about this!"

Malik scoffed. "Yes, good luck with *that*."

Peter shot him a look. *Shut the hells up!*

Further delays made sure they weren't carriers for the latest viral nasties emanating from Earth.

"But we already got checked before we left Earth."

"The elevator could've been infected, too. Now shut the hells up, Mal, or you'll get us flagged".

Eventually, they and their cargo were loaded aboard an ancient Orion capsule, repurposed for transfers between facilities like Berthold Beitz. Battered and more than a little worn, the old tug left in a series of sequential pulses pushing her into higher orbit. Peter remained strapped in, while Malik cavorted with other passengers in the tiny hold, enjoying the novelty of micro-gravity.

"Hi there." The man to Peter's left had a deep Southern drawl.

Peter conjured a cordial smile. "Uh, hello. How do you do?"

"Jon McAllister."

"Peter Hubbard."

"Good to know you, Pete." They exchanged handshakes.

"Uh, I prefer Peter. Sorry."

"Huh, you English. Always so polite. So, this your first time in space, *Peter*?"

"Yes, yes, it is. Is it that obvious, eh?"

"Well, from the way you're holding on to them there restraints, they'll have to prise your hands free with a tyre-arm."

Peter chuckled, a little tension drained.

"So, what brings you out this way? I kinda guessed you're not a tourist."

"No. I'm *en route* to Berthold Beitz, do you know it? Part of a test mission I've been developing."

"Yeah, sure. What's your field?"

"Life support systems."

"Sounds interesting. We sure need some improvement there, let me tell you. Most of these old buckets have problems adjusting to the extreme shifts in temperature, so they're always kinda hot and uncomfortable, notice that? But it's a helluva job, I tell you. What makes your new system so special?"

"I, uh…sorry, I can't really say. It's a prototype. Still under wraps."

"I can appreciate that. Me, I'm relief coordinator for the way facility in Lunar orbit."

"A 'way facility'?"

"It's kinda like a gas station, so freight to and from Mars and the Asteroid Belt can come and go, without getting too close to Mother Earth and the clutches of her gravitational field."

"I see."

"I've got me one heck of a journey ahead. I won't get there til, ooh," he glanced at the ship's chronometer, "this time tomorrow."

"Gods, that must be galling."

McAllister shrugged.

A loud buzz filled the cabin, then promptly ceased. Peter looked about in concern.

"Don't you worry yourself, that's just the EM barrier going up – uh, that'd be electro-magnetics, for the repulsive qualities it has. Don't want any of those debris particulates or micro-meteorites slamming into us now, do we? If they're small enough, they'll be deflected. No problem."

"And if they're bigger pieces?"

"Well…" McAllister crossed his eyes and let his tongue loll out.

Peter gulped.

"It's happening less frequently, but decompression's no picnic. There's only so far oxygen masks will carry you, before y'all need to get suited up."

Peter sat back and glanced out of the viewport.

Space. What the hells am I doing out here?

"But that's where facilities like your Berthold Beitz come in, am I right?" McAllister patted him on the arm. "Operation Skytrawl. Just you think about all those tugs scooping up them bigger pieces, keeping the rest of us safe. Cannibalising or throwing it back down at Earth's atmosphere, to burn up. If you think of all the garbage accumulated after all those decades of manned spaceflight, it's all gonna amount to one heck of a hazard to navigation. Not much profit to be had, so they'll be heavily subsidised. The Union of the Americas *pours* money into the endeavour. But places like your Berthold Beitz, well they'll have a nifty little side-line going on, am I right?"

"Uh, yes. I believe they retrieve older satellites in the process, along with other chunks of hardware. Service and repair them, no doubt at a premium."

"Sure thing." McAllister drove on with his dry explanation of the complexities in dealing with unwanted space debris. More than once Peter's eyes glazed over. He found himself frequently swallowing hard, and finding it difficult to breathe through his nose.

McAllister grinned. "That'll be your sinuses getting all congested. Happens in micro-g. Maybe you have that curious feeling of falling about you? Well, don't worry, if it's any consolation it ain't gonna get any worse. Lucky for you it hasn't hit you hard, otherwise you'd be spending the journey buried in a barf-bag."

Peter chuckled, not feeling particularly at ease, but he was warming to his travel guide.

"So, I hear you ask, what does a coordinator do out at the Lagrange point between Earth and Luna? Well, let me tell ya..."

Peter made a conscious effort to relax and engage more with his experience – he was in *space!* But it wasn't at all as he'd imagined, despite all the preparation and conditioning. No soaring anthems over glossy tech, like in those old picture-films; just creaking, disorientating glimpses through a grubby viewport of a dusting of stars, sprinkled over the obscured globe curving below. And a regular blinding by the Sun as their vessel rolled to dissipate heat.

He felt hot and queasy.

I could use a chill right now...I suppose there's little chance of getting one, though.

Peter managed to get a word in edgeways. "How come there's so little interactive tech aboard this craft, for passengers?"

"Well this sure ain't no pleasure craft. Many luxuries are non-existent on old buckets like this, even on some of the bigger ships. Think of it as a high frontier; you'll be lucky if your Berthold Beitz has very many of 'em. And as for full immersion, well…you can forget *that*."

"I get immerser's curse pretty bad, so it's not a problem for me."

"No kidding? Tough break. But I bet your young friend back there don't get no headaches, am I right? I bet he lives for that link. Y'see, that'll be part of the reason why, this whole trip, he's been back there fooling around with the others. Not just because of the joys of micro-g, but because there's nothing else for his mind to latch on to. So they'll play, because they can't stand the deafening silence of it all.

"At our facility, to counteract this, we've introduced a program where folk get to go under for a couple hours per day. That's all the AI resource we can spare. I sure hope your Berthold Beitz has taken up on it too, or your friend's gonna feel the squeeze. You might want to watch him on that."

Peter hadn't considered how Malik might react, going 'cold turkey'. Another aspect of this rushed endeavour that'd just got missed. His talkative companion was right, he *would* have to watch him.

The distant star of Berthold Beitz had become the outline of an orbiting facility. Peter made out the broad, box-like hangar at her base where servicing/repairs would be carried out; the rotating midsection containing rest spaces at a comfortable 0.7g; and the micro-gravity labs and docking modules protruding from her top like broccoli florets.

"Once you're on that tin-can you'll be better protected, they'll have a fierce EM barrier. And what with all them bulkheads and pressure doors, you'll be cooped up in there nice and tight."

The facility filled the viewport. Peter spotted several scorch marks, and random pitting.

So not all space junk gets deflected, then…

"See there, them geckobots? They're made in the Americas, there to carry out the kind of stuff too hazardous for humans."

54

Peter watched fascinated as silver, lizard-like creatures crawled over the facility. One emitted light from its 'beak', apparently welding something. He watched supervisory crew position themselves for their arrival, quite dishevelled-looking fellows in beat-up envirosuits.

They look more like patchworks of spare parts than proper space outfits.

He resisted the urge to wave at them.

Malik finally materialised after the call from the captain. Grinning like a child, his curly black hair floated like tree branches. He strapped himself into the spare seat next to McAllister. After a moment, he seemed to get bored and started clicking the buckle of his harness.

I wonder how long it'll be before withdrawal really hits him?

Peter sat back and tried to relax; it seemed the romance of space was passing him by.

Faster than a speeding bullet.

*

The transfer vessel docked with a shudder. It went quiet, and nobody said anything. Peter and Malik exchanged a glance.

"Uh, this'll be the point where you boys disembark." McAllister grinned. "They'll be wanting to make the next stop as soon as. Oh, and don't be forgetting your personal luggage, now. Ain't no baggage handlers out here to run around after you."

The pair made their goodbyes and floated from their seats, strapping their handheld bags on to their backs. Malik moved more gracefully; he seemed to be getting the hang of micro-g. Peter took a great deal of care to not bounce into and off things.

The vessel's tiny airlock cycled with a hiss, their ears popped and they drifted through. Although it was even warmer aboard Berthold Beitz, the smell hit them first. Despite his thick head Peter wrinkled his nose at the cross between cabbage and *must*.

It became clear that nobody was there to greet them. Peter frowned.

Are we not expected?

"Follow the yellow brick road?" Malik gestured to the bright arrows painted into the bulkheads.

They floated into the central stem, where they found some directions. Not that there was any palpable sense of 'up', but they were to head 'down' to the rotating midsection, where most of the facility's inhabitants were to be found. Malik made a *whooshing* sound as he propelled himself down the stem, twisting about.

He narrowly escaped a collision with a passing crew-member. She blew her breath out irritably, and froze him with a glare.

"Uh, excuse me." Peter drifted over. "You must be the welcoming party? It's okay you're late. We just disembarked. We're here to meet the facility coordinator. Can you take us to him, please?"

Her eyes grew several degrees cooler, and her nostrils widened. A lock of her long black hair, having escaped its pony-tailed companions, rose to form an angry antler. Her buff coveralls had 'maintenance' written down each leg, and the arms were tied about her slim waist. Peter tried to ignore her bosom which floated perpendicular to the rest of her, despite the best efforts of her sports-vest.

She cocked her head in the direction she'd come from. "You'll find him down there." Her accent was refined, but irritated. She floated briskly away.

Peter was taken aback.

Doesn't anybody in this crummy place know who we are?

They pressed on. At the base of the central stem, they faced transference on to the mid-section's rotating carousel. For a second neither knew quite how to do that. Another female crew-member emerged, her short hair floating about her broad red face. Her colourful garments did not specify a department. She held one of the grabs in the bulkhead and kept herself stationary.

"Uh, excuse me." Peter quickly orientated himself so he faced her.

"Yes, can I help you?" Her accent was German.

"There appears to have been some mistake. We're senior engineers from the mother company, and I think there's been a mix-up. We should've been met when we disembarked, just now. We don't know where to go..."

"Oh, I would not worry," she waved dismissively, "no person has time here to roll out a red carpet. I am Katja Müller, with the control guidance team. So, you are the men here to fix our life support, yes?"

"Yes, we have a conference with the facility coordinator. Could you take us to him, please?"

Katja chuckled. "Perhaps you will find Freddi at the habitation ring, someplace. With luck he is not on another rest period. Go find him. I must go now, lots and lots of work ahead of me. Perhaps I will catch up with you later, at dinner?" She smiled and was very swiftly gone.

Peter pouted.

I'm not happy being treated like this, not happy at all!

He regarded Malik, who looked troubled. "What's wrong with you?"

His assistant didn't answer; he looked far away, and his brow was furrowed.

Peter shook him impatiently. "I said, what's wrong with you, Mal?"

"I'm only getting the most tenuous interface with local AI," his voice was weak, "work rotas, emergency procedures. Some indirect comms, very little else. They seem to be blocking the rest."

"So? Maybe there's some security protocols you're not aware of, yet."

"Please wait." Malik closed his eyes.

That stoked Peter's irritation.

"All I keep getting is the bare minimum!" Malik was despairing.

"Processing power is scant enough out here, Mal, you know that. They certainly won't have resources to piss away on full immersion. I've heard facilities like this have to ration the link, but you'll get your bloody fix at some point. Just try and pull yourself together until then, will you? We haven't even started yet, and already you're falling to pieces on me. Get a grip, will you?"

He dragged Malik into the carousel, and they matched its spin. Attempting to mimic Katja's earlier example, they entered feet-first into one of the tube-like 'spokes' of the rotating habitation ring. Recollections of instructors' voices galvanised them into using the ladders, as artificial gravity took hold. They grew heavier at each rung, and after a 30-second descent they were on the curved 'ground', which sloped upwards, away, in both directions.

Peter was glad to see that this space was relatively high-tech, if not exactly pristine. A fair contrast to that old tug that had brought them here. Footsteps on the black rubber flooring caught his attention, and a pair of legs appeared from up the curving corridor. Then came the bearded face of a man, in his middle years.

"Ah, you will be Hubbard and Nayyar." The heavily accented German shook them both by the hand. "Welcome into Berthold Beitz. I am Frederik Diter, regional coordinator. You are lucky in catching me here, when I am not aboard sister facilities. I am sorry I was not able to greet you at the airlock, personally."

"I should say so!" Peter didn't try to hide his annoyance. "We had to find our own way down here. Is this how you treat all visitors to your facility?"

Frederik stared for a second, then laughed. He slapped Peter hard on the shoulder. "Ah, you are going to have fun out here, my friend! I'm afraid we give small attention to social formalities."

Peter blinked. "Nonetheless, I've had better welcomes."

"So, I am sorry." Frederik made a bow and chuckled again. "It gives us honour to have you at one of our homes, esteemed engineers from the mother company. I am your liaison with Mannesmann subsidiary, and of the facilities I oversee, Berthold Beitz is the finest. I hope your journey was acceptable?"

"Not really," Peter recalled the cramped transfer vessel, "but that space elevator really is something."

"*Ja*, the Tsiolkovsky. I have never made a journey myself, but I hear it is thrilling."

"Better than being hurled out here the traditional way, I imagine."

"It is your first time in space?"

Peter nodded.

Frederik smiled. "One day perhaps I will journey with the Tsiolkovsky, when I have enough status and importance! I will show you to the quarters when you can unpack; all of your equipments have been offloaded, so to begin work you should have few barriers."

"That's most acceptable, Frederik, thank you." Peter adapted easily to Frederik's turn of phrase, recalling his Düsseldorfer roommate as a fresher.

"How do I get a proper immersive-link?" Malik interjected, rudely.

Frederik studied him. Not his first dealings with a visitor experiencing the shock of withdrawal, his eyes held some sympathy.

"We provide allocations for periods of one hours. With time you will be assigned yours, and –"

"I would like to have mine now, please. As quickly as possible."

Peter shook his head in disgust. He exchanged a glance with Frederik.

The facility coordinator continued patiently. "We are each allocated one hours per day. If you prefer, I could organise so you have it soonest."

Peter stepped forward, deeply embarrassed at his assistant's behaviour. "Yes, that would be just great, Frederik, thank you." He shot fire at Malik. "I suppose you'd better give him my allocation, too. I won't be needing it."

He regarded Frederik and tapped his temple. "Immerser's curse."

"*Ach, so…*" Diter nodded in understanding. "I will be sure the allocations are making a pair. But it must be difficult for you, Peter, to not have at hand full resources. And please, you must call me *Freddi.*"

"I immerse when I have to, otherwise I get on just fine with my old-school tech." Peter tapped his PAD, laid mostly dormant since leaving Earth.

Frederik fell silent for a moment, studying him. "So, we must deliver your luggages. Then perhaps I will show you more, inside the facility. I can make for you the 'ten-cent-tour' as they say in the olden days, *oder?*"

Peter smiled and nodded.

There's something about this guy I like. He reminds me of Dr. Boucher, the professor's assistant during my Master's.

"So, Peter Hubbard." Frederik placed a friendly hand on his shoulder again. "You must tell me all about yourself."

*

Frederik Diter conducted a tour of Berthold Beitz, including a visit further 'down' to the micro-g hangars. He skilfully prised a great deal of information from Peter, not only about himself, but about the Deazy test programme, too.

Peter was pleased to see familiar gear on board, all from subsidiaries of AeroDomont. Especially their individual rest spaces which, although tiny, were fully equipped with stow-able tech, so they'd double as study spaces, too. Since Malik seemed to be regressing to a sulky teenager, they'd left him to indulge his two-hour immersive ration, much to Peter's chagrin. Alone now, Peter was

60

shown their primary work space, a converted area close to the control space.

Their project gear was laid out there, waiting for them.

"So this is where the famous 'Deazy' purifier is to be found?" Frederik indicated the large grey containers.

"Well, it's *all* Deazy, really." Peter took a circular walk checking everything was intact. "There's no central 'brain' *per se*, it's more a process of integrating these components with the facility's legacy systems."

"Our 'legacy' systems are just fine as they are," came a hostile voice from the hatchway. It was the black-haired woman they'd met earlier. A squat man with closely cropped hair bobbed behind her.

Frederik strode over to the hatchway, diplomatic hand extended. "Ah. Allow for me to make an introduction. Here is our head of maintenance, from our partners UniTech. Raquel Sveistrup, this is Peter Hubbard. You will be working closely together during installations and testings." He looked between them both, with some trepidation.

Peter made motions to greet Raquel, but she folded her arms in derision. "I know who he is."

Peter folded his arms too.

What accent is that? Reminds me of a German mimicking a Londoner...bet she's Danish.

"I've made it clear, Freddi, I cannot condone this –" she nodded at the gear, "this *infringement*. I have registered my disapproval."

Frederik nodded respectfully but remarked quietly, "These are men of status from AeroDomont, Raquel. We must be accommodating all of their needs." He spread his eyes and arms wide, indicating there was no choice in the matter.

The bobbing man sneered.

Raquel's antler had fallen in the artificial gravity, and she'd tucked it away behind her ear. Her icy blue eyes fixed on to Peter. "If you damage my station in any way with this toy of yours, if you risk any of us, then I will flush the whole damned thing into space. Including the pair of you two *svindlere*. Where is your assistant anyway; in hiding, I suppose?"

The bobbing man's eyes blazed. He grinned devilishly behind Raquel Sveistrup.

Peter couldn't help his frustration bubbling to the surface. "So much for the highly vaunted Danish friendliness and tolerance! I'm as pleased to be here as you are to see me, believe me."

"Excuse me?" She placed a hand on her hip.

"Look, I didn't choose to come to this 'facility'. I was ordered. There are a million places I'd much rather be right now than here. Believe me."

"So why don't you leave, then? We don't need any hack from the 'mother company' telling us how to do our jobs."

Peter added a false smile. "Maybe if you people did things properly out here, I wouldn't have to be wasting my time like this in the first place. Would I?"

"*Ach so*, maybe now we all need a little calm." Frederik tried to sound jubilant.

Peter was ready to take on anybody. "Frederik, you'll have to control these *proles* of yours. I can see I'm not welcome. But just let me do my job, and I'll be out of everybody's hair. Then you can all go back to baking in this sauna."

Raquel glared at the insult.

Peter stared back at her, haughtily.

Frederik stepped in. "Raquel, you must find a *chill* for yourself, and eat it. That is an *order*."

Raquel Sveistrup growled and disappeared, bobbing man in tow.

"Frederik, this is unacceptable. This is going to be hard enough without someone like that trying to derail me at every turn. If you can't bring your people into line, I'll have to escalate to my superiors."

Frederik's eyes twinkled but he was unperturbed. "Do what you must. Raquel has been here since the facility commissioning. You must understand she is Mother, concerned over her *Kinder*. She would make a good ally for you. You will understand it, as you work together. She is professional. Please give her some chances. And please. You must call me *Freddi*."

"Right. Just tell her to back down, okay? I was forced into coming out here, and the last thing I need is more hassle."

"You were *forced*?"

"Long story. For another time."

Frederik nodded.

But Peter felt little reassurance. Right now, all he wanted was a *chill*, and to just go home to the soothing words of Summer. Oh *hyggelig*!

*

SWITZERLAND

One day, it just 'happened'.

At her terminal in the office, Claudette Lambert sensed the Bureau's orders were ready to be unwrapped. Lurking in her mind these past weeks, the data packet had remained dormant. But now it was time.

She wouldn't be able to access their briefing directly, nobody could. Except *them*. But either way, now was neither the time nor the place. She tried to hide the intrusion while she wished her afternoon away.

She got back to her tiny allocation, and secured the place as best she could. She threw her things into the corner, strode over to the automat and took a long, deep breath. She gulped down a triple-*chill*; she'd need to be more relaxed if this was going to work properly.

By 18:30, Claudette Lambert had showered and was dressed for bed. She perched on her bunk, and took a moment to compose herself. With a sigh, she stretched out and closed her eyes. As she drifted off, she felt something 'give' in her mind. Barely noticeable, but it was there. As she slept, the secret data packet would unfurl, insinuating itself into her very dreams, the tick infecting her system.

She slept soundly, the *chills* pulling her under.

Some hours later she woke suddenly, with a start. She sat upright and massaged her temples. Instantly she recalled a dream, about one of those old picture-films from the 20th century. She couldn't remember if she'd actually *seen* the movie or whether it had been part of the Bureau's data packet; it didn't matter. But unfolding like the narrative of that old film, she now saw how things were to play out in Zug, this current assignment.

In the picture-film, two lovers from opposing houses frequently met in secret. They'd shared their innermost, stealing each other's hearts. But both were forbidden to share any of this, except with their confidante, a man who lived outside city limits.

With amazing clarity, Claudette 'saw' what she had to do. The special items she'd traced here would be passing through her supervisor's hands in the coming weeks, back at the office. When it was in their possession, Claudette was to copy all data pertaining to ESL's top secret Huldrych project, the cover name for their fifth-generation fusion-engine. She could only achieve this *in situ*, as extensive security couldn't be penetrated from the outside without being noticed.

Her jaw tightened as it became clear just *how* she was expected to store the data, once she had possession of it. She hated the Bureau even more now for this, but she kept her emotion in check. Last thing she needed right now was another painful intestoration.

Once the data was harvested, she was to execute an immediate escape plan, and head for an allocation in the outskirts of

Zürich. There she was to link with her Bureau Controller, and transfer the data over a high-security, immersive session. She would then go to ground for an unspecified period, to await further orders.

A deliberate plan of action rolled around in her mind, as she 'saw' how they wanted her to do it.

But, in the picture-film, the star-struck lovers had risked discovery. So they'd hidden far away from home, to escape those who sought to destroy them. Eventually they were met by a friend, who took care of them.

This represented Claudette's Crisis Management plan. Should she be discovered before offloading the data, she was to flee to a London safe-allocation and await interception by a Bureau officer.

Claudette recollected the twist in the tale, though, during the middle act. The lovers had become cornered by their enemies, and the man had sought answers from the heavens. He'd entreated the Christian God Himself.

Claudette's Disaster Recovery plan. Should there be a high likelihood of capture or becoming otherwise compromised, she was to link and transfer the data manually, to a final refuge. This was in fact ageing communications satellite 'ComSat07', primed to conceal the spoils in its memory core. Presumably to be collected later, by Bureau officers in low Earth orbit.

Claudette felt trapped.

Why can't they just let me transmit the stuff to that old comsat, straight away? Because they can't secure it yet. It'd still be up for grabs, that's why...

She fought the overwhelming urge to flee, while her stomach threatened intestoration. It would only be a matter of time before they would hunt her down anyway, if she were to run. Her link would act like a beacon too; only the Bureau knew how to detune them without a trace. Without a plan, support or anywhere to go, she'd be dealt with very swiftly indeed. She lacked the financial backing, too. In this reality, to properly 'disappear', you needed hard currency.

And lots of it.

Mes Dieux.

Would there be anything left of herself to save anyway, even if she did make a successful run for it?

Yes. Definitely YES.

There had to be, no matter how small a piece that may be. She had to cling on to the idea there was a place in her heart even they hadn't been able to reach. Maybe one day, when conditions were right, she'd be free of them.

Recollections of the final act surfaced. The picture-film had ended on a sombre, downbeat note. The star-struck lovers had been discovered, forced apart. In her grief, the woman had died of a broken heart. Unable to come to terms with his loss, the man had taken his own life shortly afterwards.

Claudette's blood ran cold.

The Bureau's Damage Limitation plan. If she was unable to fulfil her mission, if she faced capture, her link was now primed to trigger a brain haemorrhage.

Which would kill her.

3

RELATIONS

Several days later
LOW EARTH ORBIT

Peter Hubbard rapped irritably at the hatchway to Malik's allocation.

"Mal? Mal, are you up yet?"

He rapped again.

"Mal, it's breakfast. You need to be up now, we'll be starting work soon. Mal. *Mal!*"

Peter tutted and tapped his PAD. The 3D projection indicated the allocation's occupier was indeed present, and all seemed well with his vital signs. At least on the surface.

"Mal? Mal, let me in, come on."

Peter threw electronic notifications at him but there was still no response. He shook his head. He looked about him, saw he was utterly alone in this more remote part of the facility. He enabled the moleware buried deep inside his PAD, and effectively picked the lock to his assistant's allocation. This was the third time he'd had to do this, since coming out here.

The allocation was a mess, clothes and gear lying on the deck amongst containers part-filled with rotting food. It smelt like someone had opened a can of rotting synthetic meat and doused it with *stink*.

Malik was snoring in his bunk, an arm draped over his face. He had an amplifier attached to his temple boosting what little immersive link there was, thereby keeping him in a dreamlike state. Peter tried to remain calm. He shoved his assistant a little too hard with his foot.

Malik just lolled in the bunk.

Peter gritted his teeth and yanked the amplifier from his temple, hoping it would give him a rude awakening. Malik gasped as his eyes snapped open, and he looked about him in desperation.

"Get up. It's nearly time to start again."

Malik Nayyar whimpered.

"For gods' sakes, Mal, you need to get a grip. I can't believe you've let immersion dominate you like this. If you're not in here sulking, you're moping about like some moody teenager. Come on, get up. We've work to do."

Malik grimaced and curled into a ball.

Peter tapped his PAD and threw the ambient lighting to maximum. He shook his head. "I'm going for breakfast now, I want you to come and join me. Today's a big day. I need you."

Malik moaned and rolled over.

"I'll be at the test station as per schedule, and I expect you to be there. You'd better get your act together; that so-called head of maintenance is going to be with us today, as well."

One of Malik's feet emerged from under the covers, indicating he may actually get out of bed today.

Peter blew out a breath. "One last chance, Mal, then I'm reporting you to the professor."

This is what happens when plans are rushed, when all due considerations are left unmade. He's become about a useful to me as a choco re-entry shield.

Malik stirred again in his bunk. One eye cracked open, bloodshot, totally unrested.

Gods, he looks terrible.

Peter squatted down next to him. "Mal, seriously. You've got to get a grip."

His assistant's voice was more of a whimper. "Peter, I cannot cope. She lost it, the baby. We had a surrogate in the link, but I cannot connect. She's losing that, too."

"What are you talking about?"

"Marla. She doesn't get to stay immersed very long, these days. If she fails to nurture our son, he suffers as a consequence. As I am faced with rationing as well…it is tearing us apart, losing our baby all over again."

68

"I didn't even know she was pregnant!"

"It was a while ago. But her body couldn't sustain the foetus beyond the first trimester."

No wonder they lost it. That tech-head can barely sustain herself, let alone another life growing inside of her.

"Mal, I had no idea. You really should have said. But this immersive surrogate – it isn't *real*. Mal, you have to see that. Pining over an elaborate piece of code is *insane*."

"It is all she has."

"Well, there's nothing I can do. All I can offer suggest is that we get these installations over with as soon as possible, and you can get back to Earth and resume living in fantasyland."

Mal pulled a face and turned over again.

Am I being too harsh? No! Gods, just look at what this over-reliance on immersion is doing to the world! I feel like I could kick him right now.

Peter rose, angry. "I mean it. Get up *now,* I'm going to need your expertise. You have twenty minutes." Peter left the hatchway open as he stormed out of the allocation.

He paused in the accessway to gather his thoughts. He felt alone, frustrated. He missed his nurturing AI, and he'd not received a word from Jenn for over a week now, despite regular attempts at contact. He'd persuaded Mal to spare five precious seconds to reach out to her more directly over the link, and had even tried indirectly through her friends at work, but all to no avail.

The thought of her enjoying my status after completely discarding me really pisses me off. I miss Summer. She'd tell me everything was fine, that I'm going about this the proper way.

As Peter continued on his way, he thought about how his relationship with Frederik Diter had deepened. In the process Frederik had teased a great deal out of Peter, yet revealed very little of himself.

So what does that say about me? Gods, I'm pathetic. An orphan, first latching on to the surrogacy of AI, then the professor, and now him…I didn't know how much I needed parental guidance so badly. Not until I met this big German.

Even Raquel Sveistrup, head of maintenance, had begun to thaw as, on Frederik's blunt advice, he'd stopped trading pot-shots with her and included her in his planning. He took her concerns seriously, tried to factor them in as best he could.

But it hadn't been all airlocks and roses. Raquel's eternal sidekick, Hans Volkel, had remained openly hostile. It didn't take much of a stretch for Peter to guess why. He imagined the older man obsessing about her floating bosom, as well.

As I'm sure many others do in this place.

In lightweight AeroDomont coveralls, Peter headed for the dining space. He switched his PAD to project the day's schedule before him. The 'day' shift shared breakfast about now, and he heard rising conversation. This group occupied the middle of three fixed shifts, mirroring Europa-State time standard.

Frederik Diter bade good morning. Sat opposite Raquel Sveistrup, Katja Müller was on one side, and the ever-present Hans Volkel on the other.

Volkel rudely gestured at the projection from Peter's PAD. "Ah, our saviour has arrived. Why are you bothering with that old thing? That's '3rd World Aid' tech they would not give even to a climate refugee…Ha! Only *personal* immersion is rationed, all the official stuff is still available. *Dummkopf.*" He tapped the cheap link stuck to his temple, looking like a shiny black beetle.

It took effort for Peter to keep his mouth tightly closed.

Volkel tried again. "You don't have a link, anyway. What century are you living on?" He laughed, and looked about at the others, who kept stonily silent.

Peter regarded him coolly and tapped his own temple. "Surgically fitted, my good man. A perk of status," he continued as he leant towards him, "now just you try and remember yours. There's a good chap."

Frederik cleared his throat and eyed Volkel into silence. He asked with a curt nod, "Why don't you join us, Peter?"

"Thank you." Peter ordered black coffee and oatmeal from the automat. He couldn't shake the feeling they were all watching him. His stomach growled in anticipation of breakfast.

He sat and took a sip of coffee, grimacing at the flavour.

Volkel chuckled and Katja tutted him into silence. She regarded Peter, an earnest look on her round face. "Tell me, Peter. Does your new system extend to food preparations as well?"

"I suppose it could," he admitted, putting the coffee-like substance down. "It's primarily a climate regulator though, not a miracle worker."

"Ahhh, *schade.*"

"But we could see some effect, as systems become less burdened."

Frederik finished a mouthful of tea. "Well, perhaps in order is an overhaul of the farm anyway. What do you think, Raquel?"

She sniffed. "It's running as best it can. I'm coercing as much flavour from that algae-plant as possible, without sacrificing oxy-generation. Unless you've all found a way of giving up breathing for the rest of your tours out here?"

Frederik shrugged.

"My Deazy *could* affect flavours at source, as it were." Peter stayed diplomatic. "Do you think that might help?"

"Sure, I guess. I don't think anything like that's ever been tried, though."

"I'll get my assistant on it. It'd do him good to have something else to work on, outside our normal schedule."

Raquel shook her head. "You keep that tech-head away from my farm. Right now, I wouldn't trust him to tell me the time."

"He'll come round, you'll see. He's a talented guy."

She scoffed. "If you say so."

Peter couldn't muster an answer to that. He looked around him. "Anyway, who's up for a little trade this morning?"

Katja Müller looked up earnestly, she took her food supplements very seriously. "I have some *erdbeere* preserve left, what could you trade in return?"

"Well, I still have most of that salt left from last night. Would that do?"

Raquel puffed. "No way is salt worth the same as strawberry jam."

Peter smiled at Katja. "I hear she stockpiles the stuff; is that right, Katja?"

She grinned. "I don't know what you're talking about."

"Hmmm. So how's about this sachet of pepper I have left, too?"

"It's a deal!" Katja's ruddy face brightened even more. They made the exchange and she dusted a little of each on to her synthetic bacon and scrambled eggs, pocketing the rest. Raquel reached over and helped herself to Volkel's diminishing supply of ketchup.

Frederik rummaged in a coverall pocket and produced a small red bottle. "So, who is having items to trade for some drops of *this*?"

Katja gasped, Raquel and Volkel exchanged glances.

Peter frowned. "So, it takes tabasco to punch through to your senses now, Freddi?"

Frederik nodded knowingly. "You will see. No more will simple condiments be enough for you, with time. Then you must deploy the *big guns*. I brought this, the other day, back with me. From a visit I made to Coral Sea facility."

Peter shuddered at the thought. A fierce bartering war commenced, and Frederik laughed as he pocketed all manner of goodies in exchange for a few splashes of the fiery substance.

Peter felt a little more relaxed now. He caught Raquel's eye. "Sleep well?"

She shrugged and ate.

He smiled back.

Looking between them, Frederik placed his elbows on to the small table and rubbed his hands together. "So, Peter. You must be ready for your first installations today?"

Peter didn't look up as he stirred the jam into his oatmeal. "Yes, that's right, Freddi. Malik and I will be replacing the first legacy unit this morning and, provided all testing goes to schedule, we'll start the next installation before the week is out."

Katja screwed up her nose. "I hate that word, 'legacy'. Seems like it is for something old, worn out. Something you are *stuck* with."

Peter glanced at Raquel. "Yes, it is rather ugly and disrespectful, isn't it? I apologise."

Frederik chuckled. "Semantics. Peter, your assistant. Is he, uh, OK? Will he be joining you?"

"He's adjusting well, thanks." Peter wasn't good at lying. "I'll get him out there with me today, on the tools. That'll do him good."

"It is not an uncommon reaction in visitors, to facilities like ours who are less equipped."

"This facility's very well equipped, don't let my assistant's behaviour imply otherwise. You'll be joining us as per our plan, right, Raquel?"

She cocked her head. "Oh, I'll be there, fine. Make sure you don't screw anything up."

"That's good, because your knowledge and expertise will be invaluable." Peter didn't rise to the bait. Volkel squirmed as he shot looks between the pair of them, willing another clash.

But Peter smiled diplomatically. "Besides, I suppose you'll make sure I don't wire the thing up back to front, eh? And because you know this place inside out, nothing will go wrong if you're with me, right?"

Raquel frowned at the onus placed on to her. But she just shook her head, returning to her breakfast. Peter left it there, but

Volkel caught his glance at her bosom. The man shot him a withering look.

Peter just winked back at him. He was looking forward to catching further glances while they worked together later, in micro-g.

Hans Volkel went redder than Mars. He looked as if he was about to kill someone.

*

"She'll be here any second. Mal, are you *sure* you're going to be okay?"

Peter and his assistant were halfway up a crawlspace, bobbing in micro-g. Malik looked ghostly pale, staring down at his hands, saying nothing.

Gods, he stinks; has he even bothered to wash?

"Mal, I'm sorry you can't immerse the way you want to... the way you *need* to. I really am." He put a hand on his assistant's shoulder, who flinched. "But seriously, I need you to have my back on this, especially if she's going to be scrutinising my every bloody move. Come on, Mal, I need them old magic fingers."

Malik nodded slowly and Peter bit back his frustration. A muted thump and sounds of movement caught their attention, and Raquel Sveistrup floated into view. Peter noted a practised elegance as she manoeuvred herself into the same 'upward' position as them.

The stray strand of hair had formed that antler again, and she looked striking in her dark tee-shirt and cycle shorts. Malik's eyes bulged and his mouth fell open. He quickly looked away from her.

Raquel looked at him carefully. "It's okay, I don't bite."

Mal cleared his throat, indicating the 'legacy' components they were about to replace. "Good, it is OS9-compliant. I will be able to monitor much more effectively from the control space. Goodbye." He did an abrupt about-face and clumsily left the crawlspace, generating a cloud of dust that just hung there.

Raquel tutted, and angled the ventilation grille to disperse it.

74

Peter turned towards her. "I…I apologise for his behaviour. It's complicated."

She shrugged. "I'm surprised you let him come out here, in that state. The man's a hazard to all of us, not only himself."

"I honestly didn't know he'd be like this. Besides, I wasn't given a choice."

"So you said. Shows how much his ego relies on being propped up by AI, back down on Earth. It's a wonder he can even dress himself."

Peter felt loyalty to Mal rise in his chest, but he responded diplomatically. "I'll try to remember that. Anyway, where's Volkel? I assumed he'd be here with you."

"Someone has to run the place whilst I'm in here. And, besides, I could do without the distraction."

Right. He probably gets on her nerves as much he does mine.

"Okay, so…let's get on with it then, shall we?" He strapped a light-cam to his forehead and grabbed Malik's tool belt, left floating in his wake.

Peter didn't enjoy this filthy, lowly work but over the next few hours he completed each task with deliberate fastidiousness. He cleaned as he went, doing everything he could to show Raquel he cared about her beloved station. He fought the urge to complain about how they'd let place get so bloody dusty, and hummed quietly to himself as he worked. Eventually they were monitoring telemetry via his 3D holo, and he mumbled exchanges with Malik in the control space as the Deazy initialised.

Raquel finally broke her silence. "You married, Hubbard?"

He looked at her in surprise, although she did not take her concerned eyes off the telemetry for one second.

"No, not at all. I mean, I live with someone, my partner Jenn, but no. We're not married. We've been together a little while, we have a nice allocation…she seems happy."

Raquel cocked an eyebrow at the tone in his voice. "Work like this wreaks havoc on relationships."

"Yes. Yes, I suppose it does."

"You don't have to be so guarded with me. Not all the time."

"I know. I'm sorry."

She gestured the telemetry. "Is this accurate? We're running at almost eighty-five percent efficiency already; that's impressive."

"We should peak much higher, but around eighty-five is what I'd expect about now."

"Assuming it doesn't break, of course."

He gave her a lopsided look.

"So, you've obviously done this before, then?"

"No, at least not in conditions like this. Uh…I mean, in micro-g."

"It's okay; I don't take offence, I know this is a dusty old shit-hole. But I can see you are a skilled engineer, Peter Hubbard. Although I still don't trust you."

He nodded graciously. "So how's about you then?"

"Hmmm? What about me?"

"Are you accounted for?"

She exhaled loudly and Peter thought he'd pissed her off. "I haven't spoken to Nathaniel for, oooh…over a month now."

"I'm sorry to hear that."

Raquel smirked. "He's an asshole anyway. A total *røvhul*. You'd like him."

Peter cocked his head.

"I need to pee." She floated past, giving him a playful shove. "Let's get back to the control space, before this *legetøj* of yours breaks down and kills us all."

*

"So, how has the programme been progressing?" Frederik Diter's holo projected from the conference workspace. He was aboard another facility, joining them remotely.

It was over a week later, and Peter and Raquel were huddled around the small area of the control space. At her post, Katja Müller was monitoring the automated retrieval of some old chunk of orbital hardware. Hans Volkel was on the opposite side, fiddling with an infopanel, but listening in, for sure.

Peter assumed Malik was in his allocation, sulking. He didn't really know for definite.

"It's progressing well," Raquel activated the surface infopanel with enthusiasm, "we're almost through with phase one and we can already see – you can already *taste* – the benefits of a less-burdened system. Right?"

Frederik took in a great lungful of air. "Katja tells me it is like she is on vacation, in the *Bayerische Alpen* back home. And the food tastes better, also. I look forward to testing both, when I am next aboard."

Peter smiled but sat quietly, glad to hear others singing his Deazy's praises. In secret, Frederik had commended him on the effectiveness of his prototype and, of course, the close working relationship he'd formed with Raquel.

"I'm confident we can get system efficiency into the mid-nineties before the week is out," Raquel pored over the specs, "when we install the controlling software. *If* we install the controlling software, that is."

They both looked at Frederik.

He had gateway-sign-off of each project phase, a power of veto he was expected to exercise *especially* when critical systems were impacted. He chewed his bottom lip thoughtfully, not taking his eyes off the specs.

"Complete tasks as they are scheduled." He finally nodded. "I must arrange liaison with control. But I feel that in progressing the programme, you will have no barriers."

Raquel punched the air and Peter grinned.

"You must excuse me, by now I must be someplace else." Frederik gave them both a friendly nod and his holo dissolved.

Peter glanced over at Volkel, and caught the older man staring at Raquel. Volkel snarled as he made eye contact with Peter, who winked back.

Volkel left, stomping noisily down the accessway.

Peter blew out a breath. He kept his voice low. "So what's the deal with Volkel then?"

"Hmmm...?" Raquel didn't look up.

"He seems to have gotten himself all fired up again."

"Can't say I noticed."

"He resents me. I'm pretty sure he doesn't like the way we're working so closely together."

"Well that's his problem, isn't it?"

"It's obvious he has a thing for you, Raquel."

"I'm irresistible to the opposite sex – or hadn't you noticed? Men just can't help hurling themselves at me. The queue reaches from here to the next orbital facility."

"I bet it does. So he made a pass at you, then?"

"Yep. When he was first posted out here, shortly after me, I found he was in need of, uh… *guidance*. He's a good tech, but he needs strong leadership. He latched on to me pretty quickly and before I knew it, the *røvhul* was all but stroking my hair and worshipping me behind my back."

"Creepy."

"He'd go EVA – uh, that means 'outside' – and service the solar array without an envirosuit, if I told him to."

Peter wanted to tease but it was clear Volkel had worn her down. He gave her a friendly pat on the arm instead.

She smiled. "Still, I suppose he has a good heart. Even if he is a little deranged."

"He threatened me, you know."

"What?"

"The other day. He said if I didn't get lost and leave you alone, he'd flush me and my Deazy out the nearest airlock."

"You're kidding me."

"Nope. The guy's obsessed with you."

"Gods, I had no idea. Did you…?"

"No, I didn't get flushed out the nearest airlock."

She pulled a face. "I mean, did you take it any further, you dope."

"Oh. Nah, it's okay, I didn't get Freddi involved. I just told Volkel if he ever came near me, I'd see to it he'd never work in space again. I just needed to reassert my status; he soon got back in line."

She cocked an eyebrow at his snobbery. "Well, who's the big man, then? Do you want me to have a word with him, though, or does his lordship feel he has us proles properly in our place?"

"Oh, no, don't you dare. I've sorted it out now, no problem. Besides, I reckon having you side with me would push him over the edge."

She shook her head. "Nothing's ever simple involving people, is it?"

"Amen to *that* one. Y'know, you can engineer the ultimate concept, build the perfect system. Drop human beings into the equation, and *blip*." He snapped his fingers.

Raquel chuckled, then fell serious. "Do I really scare your assistant that much?"

"Mal? Oh, gods, yes. You frightened the life out of him the moment he saw you, that's why he runs for cover whenever you're around. First impressions and all that. But I resisted the antler'd wrath of the Ice Queen, no problem."

She elbowed him and self-consciously tucked her hair behind her ears. "Aw, come on, I was only protecting my own from you two bumbling idiots, you know that now. I'm okay once you get to know me, aren't I?"

"You're not so bad, I suppose."

She elbowed him again and sat forward, returning to the work.

Peter regarded her for a moment, in silence. She didn't deserve hassle like this. She looked strung out like so many posted in space, weary from all the psychological stress. He thought of her husband.

"Still no word from Nathaniel?"

She shook her head. "You?"

"No, I haven't heard from him either. Why would I?"

"I mean Jenn, you nincompoop."

"Ah, right. No, not a sausage. In fact, nothing the whole time I've been out here."

"Nothing even text-based?"

"She's not even bothering to open my messages now; the automatic notifications have dried up too."

"So she opened them at one point, but still didn't bother responding? That's just plain rude. Why don't you call her directly, confront her about it? Maybe at work, where you're more likely to catch her?"

"I've tried, but I get nowhere. Raquel, I'm tired of making the effort. She's made it clear how she feels, she seems perfectly happy not having me around."

"You shouldn't give up. Maybe she's hurting too? Perhaps she feels abandoned. I would."

"Sorry, but I'm afraid that's nonsense. My options were either come out here and do this, or wave goodbye to her forever. That's pretty much how she put it. AeroDomont said they'd bury me if I turned down this assignment, and she'd be gone like a shot if I lost my status."

Raquel raised both eyebrows in surprise.

"Gods know what she's up to down there, who she's with. Essentially, I'm out here so I don't lose it all. But I still can't figure out why they wanted me specifically, and not one of the seasoned test teams I originally had in my project plan."

"You seem to be handling it okay." She put a hand on his arm.

"Perhaps. But I do think being out here's doing me the world of good. I certainly don't miss her; it's liberating to actually have a clear head for once, so to speak. To actually *know* what I'm doing from one moment to the next. Not to be pulled and twisted in a billion different directions. There's something cathartic in following an immaculately structured project plan, you know."

She chuckled. "You're such a saddo. But really, it shouldn't have to be that way."

"It is how it is…we'll see what happens, eh?"

"I don't understand how you can be so flippant. Even things with Nathaniel aren't that bad. He still musters the effort to send the occasional holo, even if it's only to tell me how ill his mother still is, or how he's spending more of our money buying gadgets we don't need for our allocation."

Peter smiled. She still had her hand on his arm.

"I share your frustration, Peter. We're just not ready for space. Mankind, I mean. Despite all the training they give you, no matter how prepared you feel, ultimately we have to figure it out for ourselves. Earth-side psychologists haven't got a clue. We have to suppress our very nature living in sardine tins like this, to somehow shut off our instinctive needs and wants… There's still so much to learn about working and living out here, so much more adaptation we need to make."

"It has to start somewhere, I suppose."

"True, but I think we're going about it the wrong way. Trying to transpose Earthbound morals and mores to this hostile environment is tragically misguided. Space people can't be Earth people at the same time, it's impossible. No wonder astro-psychology is becoming the next big thing. We're not ready to be 'unleashed' out here yet. We're really not."

"So what's the answer?"

"If I knew that, do you think I'd be poking around an old wreck like this?"

"I guess not."

"I don't know, maybe those Eartherradicals are right. Maybe we should just stay put and forget the whole thing."

"You can't be serious."

"I think they have a point."

"Uh, I don't think we should be discussing this...?"

"What? Why?"

Peter jerked a thumb into the air.

"Oh you're okay out here, Peter. This AI won't go flagging you to the authorities as some kind of suicide bomber. It's too busy keeping us alive to waste processing power eavesdropping on us."

"Don't be so sure."

"Have things really gotten that bad then, back on Earth?"

"Worse. You can't even *think* it without garnering attention from someone somewhere, or from some*thing.* On our way out here, an investigative journalist managed to get himself flagged and arrested, at Clarke. Just by asking questions."

"He was researching a story?"

"Yep. I even had to shut Malik up, for being too mouthy. Otherwise we'd've been next."

Raquel pulled a face. "But that's kind of my point. We're far too immature to be let loose out here. And all those bully-boy tactics, it's all a means of control. Read Orwell, I bet the actual terrorists barely even exist. The authorities love an excuse to frighten us all into submission."

"I never had you down as a subversive."

She laughed. "I'm not. But I do think the baddies may actually have a point."

"Surely you don't think blowing innocent people to pieces can ever be justified."

"Of course not. But the underlying concept...there's something *attractive* about it."

"Perhaps. But blowing society into submission is no way to drum up membership."

"Okay, yes, their methods are deeply flawed. Misguided is not even the word. But you'd be surprised how many space-farers would agree with their principles."

"The disillusioned ones, like you?"

"*Especially* the burnt-out wrecks like me. It becomes harder justifying the huge personal cost of it all, so you wonder how it can all be worth it. But there's worse than me; just look at Volkel. He's a staunch Eartherradical, you can see it in him. Add to that his more unpredictable, fundamentalist tendencies, and…"

"Maybe you're right. Perhaps we're not ready for this, as a species. It's a shame the political and social system has grown so unwieldy; more radical views cannot be discussed peacefully without being shot down straight away."

"Well that's a whole other topic right there, for another time. But I'm growing tired of it all, Peter. I'm wondering if it's all a big novelty and one day we'll just wake up, and go home."

"At least keep me propped up while I'm out here; that's got to count for something. You seemed genuinely enthused earlier, when we briefed Freddi."

She almost smiled. "I did, didn't I?"

Peter grinned and nodded.

She sighed. "So you think it could all be worth it, in the end? If we make enough breakthroughs, if life out here can get tolerable enough…" The creases in her forehead disappeared like pulling a sheet tight across a bunk. "Maybe it's worth a try, I don't know."

"But all the while not letting those bastards back home get to you, eh?"

She smiled this time. Their eyes connected and stayed that way for more than a moment. Raquel Sveistrup flushed, and quickly withdrew her hand from his arm.

SWITZERLAND

In Zug, Claudette Lambert felt the whole office was watching her.

Of course they weren't, but it was only natural – potentially life-saving – to always assume so, particularly in her line of work. That's what made her so careful, what kept her so *alive*.

Stood at her terminal, she stretched and did the workspace pilates they'd taught her. She feigned a headache. As she tilted and moved her head, she secretly surveyed the place for watchers.

None in the physical sense, but abundant electronic snoopery, most definitely. AI would be scrutinising any and all movement, every gesture. Analysing, cross-referencing history, looking for anomalous behaviour.

She smiled, waving at a pair of co-workers leaving for lunch. Pretty soon the entire section would clear, most of them visiting the patisserie at the end of the *Strasse*.

A quick glance confirmed her supervisor's terminal was also empty, he was lunching too. She knew the Huldrych data was on his system right now; files on their 5th generation fusion-engine. The very ones she'd been planted there in the first place, to steal.

She also knew she'd miss her window of opportunity if she didn't make her move. Now was time to execute the deliberate plan of action, which had been rattling around in her mind for what felt like an eternity.

As cover, she grabbed the tablet she knew her supervisor wanted from her. She also took her favourite mug. But first she moved to the small dining space, where the automat dispensed a *heisse schokolade* blended with as many soothes as would elude an AI flag. She'd need the painkilling supplement for what she was about to do.

She sipped at the mahogany liquid; it tantalised her taste buds like velvet magma igniting her innards.

Full immersion was unofficially frowned upon whilst at work, unless of course on company business. But her link had been malfunctioning all morning, just like she'd programmed it to. So dialling the temporal device down to almost nothing went unnoticed, seemingly another malfunction. She gave it a moment, then, through an act of will, disabled it completely.

Now she was off-grid. Not even AI could track her over the link. But it could only last a short while before a flag popped up somewhere.

She blew on her hot drink and drew mouthfuls of the thick, sweet substance. Lightheadedness followed as the soothes kicked in early, while she left the dining space for her supervisor's workspace.

Patton's space was silent, eerie. Was there some kind of immersive dampener? Probably. She dropped the tablet on to his workspace and set her mug down, pressing it hard on to the glassy surface. She spent a moment flicking through the tablet's content, as if double checking some important detail. Then she left the space, remembering to clean the wet ring her mug had left behind.

She pretended she needed to pee. Facilities were close-by, so she may as well take her mug with her.

Surveillance was forbidden in a wet space. Not even Ephersyn-Stoffel-Lauter, the world-renowned fusion-engine Goliath, could watch their minions urinate. Europa-State authorities would not allow it, at least not officially anyway. But she couldn't assume she wasn't being monitored some other way, even temporarily off the immersive grid as she was.

She entered a cubicle, pulled down her panties, and sat. She balanced the warm mug between her thighs, its contents all but gone now.

A certain twist of its handle revealed a fine, silk-like thread.

The mug was more than a mere vessel for hot chocolate. Its crystalline structure now held ESL's most secret information, the Huldrych files. She'd calculated her fool supervisor would leave them unprotected for a period as he left to fill his stomach, making the data an easy target. And those files would only be on the site servers for twenty-four hours. That's why today had had to be the day.

She extended the thread and attached it to her link. With a thought, she initiated a connection.

Years ago, when she entered Bureau09 service, Claudette Lambert had undergone a series of gruelling operations to pattern her brain for data storage. A fine silicon/organic meshing. These days most people could hold everything they needed in their links, sure. But she had an advantage over the rest; she could keep it all locked inside, utterly secret no matter what.

Her mind adapted, chemically sorting the data in such a way only fragments would ever be recovered, even after the most invasive surgery. And Claudette Lambert had grown quite attached to her brain. So through a series of almost meditative steps, she'd learned to categorise and encrypt data which would remain dormant until called for.

The only downside was a neuro-chemical one. Once synaptic contacts had fused, she had no way of maintaining them in the field. Which meant that, over time, data integrity would slowly degrade.

The transfer from mug to mind was relatively swift; organics were always so much *better* than hard tech. Faster than it had taken to haul the files from her supervisor's terminal, at least, and that could be measured in seconds.

She'd had her eyes closed the whole time. When they finally parted, the pain was almost instant; light burned. It always did after this.

She let go of the thread. She'd constructed her mug to be particularly susceptible to the hydrochloric acid they put in chemicals to clean these toilets, so its constituent parts would dissolve when making contact. And all that classified data it held would be lost, too.

She parted her legs, the mug *sploshed* into the water and began to disappear almost immediately. Claudette Lambert rose, flushed and straightened herself up. Passing from the wet space into the open plan office, she winced inwardly at the brightness of the lights, the mood-walls seemingly pulsating now.

She daren't show this openly. AI would be obsessing over any anomalous behaviour, and Claudette Lambert was always ultra-careful.

She opened her link and reconnected. In an instant, she just *knew* what time it was. Lunchtime, of course! She gathered her stuff, remembered her raincoat. Then outside, the crisp Swiss air reminded her spring had not fully sprung.

She gathered her collar around her face at the stiff breeze. At least it wasn't raining. She strode, heading for the patisserie on the corner where everybody else was. When she was outside the permissible corporate net, she'd execute her escape plan, walk right on past the place, and keep on walking. Just like those starstruck lovers had done, in that old picture-film. She'd need to grab her holdall, the one she'd left at the *bahnhof* the night before.

But, alas, she hadn't been careful enough.

Back at the office, AI had flagged the fact she'd left the wet space without the mug she went in with. Security were already notified, agents were on their way in there, to check. They were casually expecting to retrieve the vessel and put it back on her desk, but when they came up empty...

It was only a matter of time before all hells broke loose. Claudette Lambert would soon be a most wanted person.

4

TRUST

LOW EARTH ORBIT

That afternoon, Peter and Raquel were in the staging area unpacking the next sequence of gear, as part of the second test installation.

Raquel regarded him. "Are you sure he'll be okay in there, all by himself?"

"Who, Mal? Yeah, he'll be fine. He's only prepping the next instal, and I don't really need to be there for that, although according to the plan I'm *meant* to be. I'll head over there shortly once we're done, and I'll check on –"

The blaring alarm-klaxon stopped him mid-sentence. They both looked dumbstruck at each other for a moment, wondering what in the solar system was going on. But the noise wasn't going away.

Raquel bolted for the infopanel; she had to yell over the din. "It's a proximity alarm! One of the autotugs is coming in hot!"

She ran out the hatchway. Confused, Peter followed her.

They made it to the control space. Frederik was bent over Katja Müller's workspace, where she was frantically tapping her infopanel.

"Freddi, what the hells is going on?" Raquel leant in to take a look.

Frederik barked over the noise. "It is an autotug we cannot control, he has entered our space but with thrusters sticking at full. He is hauling a mass of more than two tonnes."

"Why haven't the fail-safes kicked in?"

"I do not know, we have no control."

"Is it outside the EM barrier?"

"Yes." Frederik held both hands over his ears. "Halt that sound, please, someone!"

Katja nodded and the alarm-klaxon fell silent.

Raquel moved to another infopanel, and went in under her maintenance passcode. "Looks like the retros are misaligned; they think they're decelerating the 'tug when in fact they're *accelerating* it, towards us. The greater the alarm gets to, the harder the retros burn. At this rate it'll crash into the facility in less than one minute!"

"*Scheisse*...I will know where he will hit. *Jetzt!*"

Katja pounded at the infopanel. "I-I cannot calculate point of impact – the vector is not constant!"

Raquel tapped away. "All the thrusters are pulsing to compensate, direction is becoming erratic. One moment...Likeliest point of impact will be up near the docking modules, outer module Z-13."

Frederik tapped Katja on the shoulder. "Is any facility crew in this place?"

She shook her head. "No. According to the schedules all personnel are either here with us, or down in the hangar."

Frederik gritted his teeth. "Close bulkheads. Seal all hatchways."

Katja nodded. "Done."

Like all sections of the facility, the control space was now isolated to protect them from potential decompression.

"Wait!" Peter stepped forward. "OMZ-13? That's where my next test is supposed to be, right?"

Frederik frowned. "Peter, we cannot let your –"

Raquel cut in. "Gods, he's right. His *assistant's* in there right now, prepping the place!"

Frederik's jaw fell open as he looked at the data. AI indicated an active link in the module. The ident was Malik's.

Katja's voice broke. "Impact in twenty seconds."

Peter grabbed Frederik by the arm. "You've got to give him a chance to get out of there! Katja, can you raise him over the comms?"

89

"Negative, he is unresponsive." Katja continued the countdown to impact.

Peter pleaded. "Freddi, give the man a chance to get away from the outer modules, at least! He's trapped in there!"

Frederik shrugged Peter off. "It is too late. There are rules. The whole facility I cannot put in risk, for one man. I am sorry, Peter."

Katja counted down to zero.

Nothing happened, and for a brief moment Peter thought they'd got their sums wrong.

And then the autotug, laden with two tonnes of orbital hardware, slammed into Berthold Beitz.

The alarm-klaxon shrieked again, and the deck shook beneath their feet. As they lost power, infopanels and screens went dead. Emergency lighting flickered on, casting an eerie blue glow.

Frederik barked. "Everybody, suited up. *Now*. Facility-wide messaging!"

Katja nodded as sections acknowledged the order.

The facility shuddered again as emergency response fired retro-thrusters to counteract the impact, to maintain a stable orbit. The habitation ring slowed, its rotation coming to a stop.

"Again, silence the alarm!"

"Done!"

"The autotug, what is his status?"

"It's floating free, the retros are spent."

"Later we will deal with him. But heat will be leaving us soon, also," Frederik warned.

Micro-g fell, and things began to float upwards. Raquel took hold of Peter and pulled him toward the emergency lockers. "It's okay, I'm sure he's fine. If we suit up, we can reach him. That hatchway would've sealed him in tight."

Peter shook his head in bewilderment.

"He'll be safe in there, we can get to him."

"We can't know that for sure."

"We'll make him our priority." Raquel called over to Katja. "Kat, are all other crew accounted for?"

"Affirmative."

They yanked on their envirosuits, knocking clumsily into one-another.

Frederik initiated the suits' comms. "Katja, what is AI status?"

She closed her eyes and immersed, linking with the facility's central brain. "It's there. But I have no telemetry at the point of impact."

Raquel turned to Frederik, waving away gear that now floated before her. "We'll work our way up from here, clearing each section as we go. You'd better take Volkel and head downwards, towards the hangars. Where the hells is he, anyway?"

Frederik shrugged.

Katja was strapping herself into the seat at her workspace. "I show him in the rest allocations."

Raquel nodded. "Right. Is the pressure holding on the other side of this hatchway?"

"It is."

"Good. Tell him to come meet us in the accessway, then."

Due to loss of power, they had to manually crank the hatchway. Volkel was already on the other side, already envirosuited, helping them get it open.

"Good, Hans, you're here. Go with Freddi." Raquel was the first to float through. "I need you to check this section and the hangar. I'm heading up to the outer modules, there's at least one person trapped up there."

"Understood." Volkel was sweating, his eyes fixed on Raquel's. But he did a double-take, then gold-fished as Peter floated through behind her.

Peter tutted, shaking his head.

Gods, not now, you ignoramus. Last thing I need is you and your petty jealousy!

91

"Give me regular updates," Raquel called behind them as she pulled Peter away. "Keep a channel open at all times. Once we're done with the interior, we'll need to check outside. Katja, keep an eye on that rogue autotug! You'll have to muster a team to manually secure it."

They made it to the now-stationary carousel, and Katja confirmed that pressure was holding on the other side of the hatchway they needed. They manually opened it and floated easily up the facility's central stem, towards the docking modules.

"He would've been in one of the crawlspaces, at OMZ-13." Peter sounded breathless.

"Those are all situated along the outer-hull. Triple reinforced to brace against micro-meteorite impact."

"But not against an out of control autotug with a hefty satellite in tow, I bet."

Raquel didn't, couldn't answer.

As they floated up the stem, Raquel made OMZ-13 their first port of call. The docking module itself was inactive, but they clambered in to get a look through the viewports to the crawlspaces. The port-side was pressurised, but empty. The starboard-side was depressurised, and occupied.

Craning to get a good view in his envirosuit, Peter caught a glimpse of the interior.

There was no evidence of a puncture to the outer wall, so perhaps a joint had ruptured. But his assistant Malik was in there, fine.

Curled up, bobbing in the foetal position amongst other floating debris.

Although airless now, the crawlspace itself would still be holding some heat, so the intense cold of the shade hadn't affected him yet. But the lack of air had finished him off.

As he'd suffocated, hard vacuum had pulled blood vessels to the surface of his skin, which itself had lost its colour. Malik Nayyar looked like he'd been overlaid by a patchwork of criss-crossing, purple branches.

Peter gasped. "Gods, Mal..."

"Oh no." Raquel sucked in a breath, and held it.

*

SWITZERLAND

Claudette Lambert hadn't banked on growing a tail so soon.

She was marked for sure, so plans had changed. She'd received a message to abandon her rendezvous in the outskirts of Zürich, and initiate the crisis management plan. She had to get to London.

So, she'd headed West to Lucerne, deeper into Switzerland.

It was a brisk evening, and she had her raincoat pulled tight around her waist, its high collar round her face. Her heels pounded the cobbles as she strode along the banks of the serene Vierwaldstättersee. On the outside her posture was neutral, but inside Claudette's head, turmoil raged. She forced herself to not clutch her holdall so tightly, but her mind throbbed with Huldrych data.

Her bag contained a number of contingency IDs, from sweet old Gramma to dusty spinster. Now it seemed disaster was more likely to strike, each ID had a part to play in getting her to safety.

Claudette's link fought hard to partition the raging torrent cascading inside her skull. Typically, data would become useless after 120 hours. She doubted her sanity would extend 120 *minutes* at this rate. She had to get this data-jam out of her head, double-damn quick.

Claudette left the stretch of Vierwaldstättersee, in the opposite direction to the Hauptbahnhof, and doubled-back. Despite her distracted mind she noticed for the second time the dark-suited figure following in her footsteps. She quickened her pace and crossed the Strasse, taking an immediate sharp left into a quiet alleyway.

The figure followed her into the mouth of the alley. It didn't matter if they were ESL security, or some other third-party keen on what was in her head.

She'd been rumbled.

Claudette Lambert began to run.

*

LOW EARTH ORBIT

Malik Nayyar could not be revived.

It took time – too long – before they could create a backstop to maintain facility-wide pressure, haul him free from the crawlspace, then re-pressurise OMZ-13. Raquel tried everything she could, even Frederik had gotten to them with resuscitation gear. But they'd passed the threshold, entailing brain death.

With all reverence possible in the cramped environment, they'd placed him into a bodybag and secured him in the facility's tiny, emergency treatment space. He would be shipped back to Earth on the next supply run.

And then Peter's blood began to boil.

"Peter, you must control yourself!" Frederik held Peter, to stop him going off on a rampage.

"I'm gonna *kill* that bastard," Peter spat. "It was him! He sabotaged that 'tug, programmed it to deliberately crash into us!"

"Hans Volkel, you mean? It is mad."

"Get your hands off me, Freddi, I want to claw his gods-damned eyes out!"

Frederik did not let go. "But *why* would he do something like this?"

Raquel helped restrain him. "Peter, listen to me. You need to calm down."

"Raquel, you know why. How jealous he's been of *us*. He thought I was in that module too – you saw how he reacted when he saw I wasn't!"

"You're being irrational, Peter, you need to take a few deep breaths."

"But am I, though? Am I really?"

"Even with his petty jealousy, I can't imagine him resorting to something like this! He could've finished us all, not just you."

"He did it for the attention, don't you see? And maybe that was his plan all along. His mandate. You said it yourself, you think he's an Eartherradical. His behaviour having been somewhat erratic of late? If AI here was up to it, he would've been spotted sooner. Maybe he was *assigned* to disrupt things as much as possible, out here. And taking me out too, well – that would just be a bonus."

Frederik eyed her. "Raquel, what is this?"

"Oh, come on! Sure he's been behaving like an ass these past couple of weeks, but it's hardly conclusive proof, is it? I can't imagine him actively sabotaging the one and only place that keeps him alive, out here."

"He stayed well away from the habitation and workspaces, didn't he? Only singled out that one place he thought Mal and I would be in?"

"You're crazy."

"Oh yeah?" Peter was nodding fast. "He'd gotten suited up quick enough as well, hadn't he? And was that surprise on his face, right after the crash? Not his usual disdain in seeing me?"

Frederik tutted and increased his grip on Peter, squeezing some sense into him.

"This is all interesting, these stories. One evening we listen over cocoa. But I suggest we leave them until another time, we must get the facility back online until, maybe, we all die? Shall we do that, yes?"

*

Raquel took Peter up on his offer of lending his expertise to the repair effort, although it was an extra burden keeping him away from Volkel.

As they surveyed the facility, making repairs, other crew members manually towed the faulty autotug into the hangar, and cordoned it off on Frederik's orders. The next job was to correct Berthold Beitz' orbit, and get the habitation level rotating again. Only when facility-wide damage had been brought under control did they seek further answers.

Raquel returned to the micro-g hangar and retrieved the unit's 'brain', its card-cage. Frederik gave her time and space to inspect the hardware personally while, for the time being, Peter was confined to allocation – 'for his own safety'.

After some time, Raquel found an anomaly that deeply disturbed her.

She called for a closed meeting with Frederik and Peter, in her personal allocation. She was the first to speak. "The port-dorsal thruster assembly had been programmed to rotate 180° upon approaching the facility, and the lines of code normally triggering autocorrect had been corrupted. As a result, attempts at failsafe just left the processor hanging, for a checksum that never came. It was done with a great deal of care. I nearly missed it.

She looked up at the facility coordinator. "Freddi, I cannot put this down to a 'glitch'. It was no billion-to-one programming error, either."

Frederik's eyebrows rose, in unison. "Are you saying it was deliberately created? Someone made this sabotage to the autotug?"

She glanced at Peter, the strain of recent events had turned her eyes a milky-grey. She nodded, grimly.

Peter shook his head. "I bloody knew it."

Frederik raised a cautionary hand. "Maybe it was any person in this room, who made the changes. Maybe it was any person out there, who also did it. We do not know at this stage."

Raquel cleared her throat. "Well, apart from myself, and those present...Hans Volkel has the technical know-how, and –"

Peter rose. "I told you! Freddi, I demand he is apprehended. Immediately!"

Frederik tutted and sat him back down again. "The screening is a long process, Peter. A psychopath could not be out here, so easily."

"I bet your AI isn't as paranoid as those Earth-side."

Raquel raised her voice to get them back on track. "*So* I looked into the logs. AI had a ghost of all past registrations with the sabotaged unit. It was definitely Hans Volkel, no mistake."

Peter went scarlet. "Bastard!"

Frederik shot him a look.

Raquel continued. "He did a very thorough job covering his tracks; like I say, it took some digging. What the hells are we going to do now?"

Frederik placated Peter with a nod. "We must arrest him. Before he can make, for us, more problems."

Raquel stood, nodding. "Agreed. Let's go."

Frederik stood in front of the hatchway. "No. It is better you two stay here. I must get cargo haulers, for help, I will need muscles. I will call when I have answers."

"At least, let me help you," Peter rose again, "for Mal's sake."

"Peter," Frederik stood an inch away from his face, "you-will-*sit.*"

Peter clenched his jaw.

Frederik snapped his fingers signalling Raquel, she guided him back towards the bunk again.

Forcing calm, Peter sat. "Well, when you *do* have him, make sure the bastard's secure. I don't know what I'd do if I ever saw him again. Besides, he may want to make another attempt on *my* life."

Frederik agreed, a curt gesture with his whole body yet somehow with minimal movement. He left, soft-locking the hatchway so no-one else could enter without their permission.

Raquel flopped on to the bunk. She regarded Peter for a moment.

"I'm sorry, Raquel. Mal didn't deserve to get caught in the crossfire like that."

"It's okay." She extended an arm around him.

"Thanks for everything you've done."

"No problem."

"I can't believe it. How could anybody do this?"

She held him closer. "It beggars belief. Did he have much family, back home?"

"His parents are still in India, a brother somewhere in the Americas. He lived with his girlfriend, Marla, in our complex. Gods know how she's going to take it. The loss will be one thing, but she was so *reliant* on his status, for the link. You thought he was a tech-head? He was the model of sobriety, next to her."

"She's going to suffer then."

"I'm afraid so. It'll probably finish her off. I'll do my best, but I don't know what *could* get her through this. Not like I can rely on Jenn to watch over her, is it? She's nowhere to be seen, either…"

"How frustrating."

"I'll make my report to my superiors, shortly. It's up to them to let her know about Mal, not me. I don't think his plan would cover her, for mental health. She wasn't an official spouse or anything, I don't think he ever registered her. Like I did with Jenn."

"That's tough. Maybe she has family who can take her in?"

"I don't know."

A moment of silence while she held him.

He stirred. "You know, it's curious. A moment ago I wanted to tear out Volkel's windpipe, but now I feel…I don't know. I suppose I've never been in a situation like this before."

"It's shock, you're exhausted. It is okay to feel nothing, you know."

"Perhaps. I just keep wondering how this will impact my project. If I'll ever get off this tin can. What kind of person does that make me?"

"That's a sick joke. But at least you're honest."

"Yes. Anyway, do you still side with the Eartherradical crazies, after all this?"

"We still don't know if Volkel actually was one."

"Security AI will get to the bottom of it. Scour his brain, it will, until he won't even be sure what his own name is. I've read about it in the newsfeeds. But it just goes to show you were right, though."

"Right, about what?"

"About us. We're really not ready, are we? For life out here. Mankind's got a lot of growing up to do before we can even *think* of settling out here, permanently."

She chuckled. "Tell that to the thousands of settlers on Mars, not to mention the Moon, the Asteroid Belt, and all the facilities in-between…"

"So we're doomed, then."

"Yes, doomed to repeat it all again. And that's mankind's way, just stick your nose in any history book. But y'know, I've become so *weary* of this, I feel like something's been scooped right out of me. Stretches of mindless tedium, then blind panic to avert some mind-bending disaster. We could've *all* died back then, do you realise that? Not just Mal. You know how you're feeling numb right now? That's been me, pretty much since coming out here. The pretence that everything's fine really saps your energy – I'm spent, I really am."

"I don't know how you've coped so long. I've only been out here five minutes, and I'm already one step away from pushing a man out of an airlock."

"It's tough. But as usual we have to put up, and shut up. In our own way. Nobody tells you how to do it. There's no-one really to reach out to, because no-one wants to hear it. No-one wants to *face* it. We're all in the same boat, frightened of admitting the same thing."

"That we should write the whole thing off as a bad idea, and just go back home?"

She fell silent for another moment, and they held their embrace.

Peter sniffed. "You suppose Freddi and his heavies have sorted out Volkel yet?"

"They must have, by now. He did say he'd message us. I'll pop out in a minute, check if all's clear."

"There's no rush."

He laid his head on to hers. She rested her hand on his leg. Her little finger grazed the top of his inner thigh, and stayed there.

Raquel squeezed.

*

TRANS-LONDON

The clock was ticking. For two days now the stolen data had rattled inside Claudette Lambert's skull.

She'd evaded her pursuers in Switzerland only by taking a massive detour into Italy, switching IDs to throw them off the scent. Then her escape plan had taken her north-west, across France, then back towards the United Kingdom.

Unrecognisable through her disguise, hunched in a seat aboard the bullet-train connecting mainland Europa-State to London. Her jaw ached through constant clenching, her attention flitted in rapid, bird-like movements. Dressed as a matriarchal figure, easily eighty years of age, she chided herself for not behaving like Gramma would have done, but she was starting to lose control. The dull passenger sat opposite kept glancing at her, wondering.

No doubt her opponents would have zeroed her by now if they'd also boarded the train, so the fact she was still alive was some solace. She allowed herself to sit back in her seat.

At least that's something.

She closed her eyes, ostensibly pretending to doze, but in reality, fighting to maintain a grip on her mind.

She shifted her focus on to her breath and elongated each exhale, moving them from her chest to the pit of her stomach. After a moment she moved her awareness down to her feet. This calmed her somewhat. She couldn't maintain this meditative state very long, but she kept going back to her breath, and tried again.

Not long now before St. Pancras terminal. Just stick with it. I can see the route to the Bureau's safe-allocation, mapped out in my mind.

She allowed her focus to dull as the train gently rocked her to and fro. Sensing her exhaustion, her link discretely kicked in, helping soothe her beleaguered mind into rest.

Claudette Lambert dozed. She dreamt of old-fashioned filing cabinets, bursting open with paper files.

She awoke with a start as the train rolled to a halt. The onboard crew announced their arrival in London. She hadn't realised she'd fallen into such a deep sleep and she sat bolt upright, the passenger opposite smirked at poor old Gramma as they gathered their things.

Claudette worked her jaw and looked about groggily, summoning her link to jolt her fully awake. She hauled herself off the train, forcing herself to fix her focus on the back of another disembarking passenger and not look too obvious.

AI would be red-hot; it would flag flitting eyes, unusual body language and short breathing to local security. She'd have a tough time denying she was an Eartherradical, let alone explaining away her disguise, to them.

She feigned fiddling with her holdall near the public wet spaces, loitering until someone with the right attributes came along. She spotted a bespectacled, middle-aged woman approaching, and tried her best to study her body language as she followed her into the over-lit, gender-neutral wet space.

Claudette glanced about, seeing they were alone, and shoved her into a cubicle. She held the startled woman's mouth closed, and linked with her. Predictably her security settings hadn't ever been updated, so via direct-send Claudette triggered a sleep command that short-circuited her mind into unconsciousness.

She swapped clothing with her victim, adding the Gramma wig and spectacles, and after a moment the spinster alternate-ID emerged. As per the backstory Claudette had hurriedly created, she played the part of a lonely singleton whose self-confidence was at a low ebb. Now her nervous, fidgeting energy would suit this profile to a tee.

Claudette exited St. Pancras terminal. She'd quite forgotten how packed London could get. Commuters pushing, shoving, non-verbally complaining about the incessant rainfall and overcrowding by screwing their faces up against the world. Londoners would hiss, spit, but never talk to one another. The wailing and screams came from gangs of climate refugees, harassing people for credits.

She'd been to London several times before, which should've informed her sense of 'normal' in spotting anomalies, but the place was so congested she could barely move. She joined the throng which carried her east to an autotram space. After waiting far longer than planned, she squeezed on to one of the public conveyances, heading east.

Claudette sensed she wasn't being followed. Nonetheless she changed trams once more, taking her on a diagonal route to Hyde Park. There she boarded a final tram, taking her all the way back east again, to the docklands.

It was getting late, the obscured Sun had long since set and the wet night was drawing in. Claudette hopped off the autotram one stop early. With caution drummed into her by long years of experience, she reconnoitred the tall, glistening block from a distance. The safe-allocation was on the 3rd floor. Indications were all that she was safe, with no tail, and her sanctuary hadn't been compromised either.

She approached the main entrance, trying to maintain character as she walked through the glassy reception. She rode the elevator. After a short walk along the carpeted accessway, the door to #14 clicked open, sensing who she was.

Inside the safe-allocation, all was still, completely silent. Claudette allowed herself a long exhale as she triple-bolted the door behind her. She stood straight, shaking off the spinster alternate-ID and stretched her neck, her back, in a series of jarring clicks and cracks.

She turned and entered the allocation proper; all seemed well until she was blindsided by a blow to the face. Presumably meant to knock her out, the strike hadn't been planted correctly and Claudette merely stumbled. A figure wearing a full cloaking-suit, an active mesh that made them immersively 'invisible', was upon her. Claudette spun round and extended her right arm, winding her attacker, but the force of the onslaught sent them both crashing into the wall.

They tussled, Claudette recovering from the attack and desperately trying to regain her focus. She landed several blows, but her assailant span and planted a foot directly into her left side. Claudette yelped in pain.

She went down and managed to roll away from them, further into the allocation, but her attacker was instantly on her again. Claudette withstood the blows, summoned every ounce of strength she could, and hauled herself up. Deflecting the attack by bear-hugging her assailant, she used their combined bodyweight and the force of their onslaught to send them both crashing into the dining space.

It hadn't registered with Claudette just how slight her opponent was, but with the right kind of skill such proportions were meaningless.

Claudette got to her feet, gritting her teeth in a bloody mouth. She ran at her enemy, grabbing the first thing she came to, tearing a gash in the hood of the cloak. A lock of crimson hair tussled through the gap and, snarling like an animal, Claudette tore viciously and wrenched a handful from its roots.

The attacker emitted a high-pitched scream, Claudette continued to tear at her assailant's hair, their face. She gasped in surprise as she fell over something, causing them both to land painfully. A quick glance confirmed she'd tripped over a corpse, presumably her Bureau09 rendezvous.

Damn! The agent I was meant to have finally shared this logjam in my head with...

This angered Claudette as it dawned on her the situation was much further beyond her control than even she realised; with her 'back-up' confirmed down, if she was captured now or otherwise incapacitated, her link would trigger a fatal brain haemorrhage.

I'm not ready to die. Not after all I've been through!

So she fought her attacker, literally tooth and nail. The fight had become so bloody and ugly, Claudette did everything she could to stay alive. Her attacker was well trained, but so was she. Eventually she knocked her adversary unconscious, by ramming the ailing figure head-first into the manufactarium.

Claudette propped herself against the entrance to the dining space, her breathing coming in painful gasps. Her clothing was ripped to shreds, blood – both hers and the attacker's – was everywhere. She gathered herself; there was little time left. She had to act, right now.

It's a mystery how this place became compromised. So they would have trailed me discreetly since France, knowing I could easily be intercepted here. Which means there'll be more of them coming.

Her final option was to link with ComSat09 in low Earth orbit, upload the degrading data-monster from her head, and get the hells out of there.

Claudette closed her eyes and executed an immersive link. She thought about the closing sequences of that old picture-film, the forbidden lovers doomed to an inevitable death, far apart from one another. The Bureau's immersive programming did the rest.

She *saw* the path to ComSat09, way out there in space. She *felt* its cold surfaces as she ran down its crystalline memory core. She *saw* there was ample space, she wasted no time dumping the leaden chunk of data that'd weighed her down for so long. She shuddered in exhilaration as its poison was drawn out of her, in a torrent of data.

The transfer felt quick, but was nonetheless efficient. She felt liberation too as her mind became gradually more spacious, free of the monster she'd been carrying this whole time. She let out a long cry of relief.

But then something felt wrong, very wrong.

Claudette Lambert frowned, her jaw slackened and she emitted a small moan. Then slumped involuntarily to the floor like a rag-doll. Completely motionless, fresh blood oozing from her eyes, her nose, her ears.

Her controller at the Bureau had omitted one important detail in her mission parameters. Once she'd uploaded the data, following a sense of temporary elation, she'd always been doomed to suffer this final fate. To ensure complete deniability, her link had always been programmed to kill her at this point, whether she'd been compromised or not.

Although somewhat degraded by now, the data harvest was safely ensconced aboard an ageing communications satellite, in low Earth orbit. Now dormant, waiting to see which side got to the stolen bounty first.

The game was afoot.

LOW EARTH ORBIT

Days passed, and a relationship developed between Peter Hubbard and Raquel Sveistrup. A hand on a thigh became an embrace; an embrace a fleeting kiss.

Mal was due for repatriation to Earth any moment, via one of the frequent autotugs. The snarling Hans Volkel had been confined to allocation, awaiting a supervised, manned vessel for his return journey. He'd spat his innocence every inch of the way, but Frederik kept him in restraints and AI maintained rigorous surveillance.

Somehow, life found a semblance of normality aboard Berthold Beitz.

Deazy installations resumed. Peter and Raquel worked more closely than ever, and also spent more of their spare time together.

Then the moment came when human nature could no longer contain itself. Raquel handled all the details. She knew the facility, the work rotas, far better than he did. After all, it was *her* place. She instructed Peter to rendezvous at the micro-g 'bottom' of the facility, ostensibly to survey the area for the next phase of their installation schedule.

But she had something else in mind, entirely.

She led him to the huge hangar complex, where satellites were stowed for repair and servicing. A place Peter had only been once, during his entire time aboard the facility.

The whole area was quiet, a rest period, the next shift not due on for almost an entire rotation.

"An autotug's due, in about an hour," Raquel tapped a maintenance shortcut into the infopanel, "but we'll still be alone. There won't be anyone around needing to check it in. But still, just in case…"

She set the zone sensors to a diagnostic cycle, effectively masking their presence. She glanced over her shoulder to check they were completely alone, and took Peter's hand. She led him into the control booth where crew would oversee depressurised hangar operations. Raquel closed the hatchway behind them; eerie infopanel glow was their only source of illumination.

"I assume you've never done this before," she whispered, pulling him close as they floated, "I mean, in micro-g?"

He shook his head.

Her eyes teased playfully. "I'd better drive, then."

She smiled as she stripped off her vest, and pulsating tones and strawberry eased from her bra.

Peter smiled back in approval. "I don't imagine you get to wear *that* very often out here, the carewear version I mean."

"Mmmm, just the regular ones." She smiled again. "It's a disgrace, it really is."

From a pocket she retrieved a tube, the kind they put food in. She squeezed a generous helping of its translucent content on to her finger, spreading it thickly over her lips. She drew him to her and kissed, sharing the substance while their tongues entwined.

Peter recognised the immediate rush of concentrated bright, the stimulant.

Not that I particularly need any extra energy right now, but a boost will certainly come in handy...

She untied her long black hair, and it rose around her slim face like a peacock's plumage. She pushed him into the corner and wrapped his wrists around a pair of hand holds, lodging one of his feet against a protruding vent in the bulkhead.

"Hold tight," she unzipped his coveralls, "I mean, one of us has to...otherwise this can be *disastrous*."

The session was intense, and very different. The lack of gravity added a new dynamic, while Raquel stoked his libido over the link. Not immersion enough to trigger a headache in him, just tantalising fondles so they could *feel* each other in the most subtle, sensual way.

Oral sex led to a second session. But as they continued to make love, neither of them noticed Frederik Diter enter the control booth.

The game was up, they all knew it. As they disengaged nothing was specifically said, Raquel just mumbled some nonsense about essential maintenance. Of course Diter was discreet enough not to enquire what *type* of routine maintenance would need them both to be half-naked, and rutting like newlyweds.

Raquel left the booth very quickly. Frederik gave Peter a sly wink and a hearty slap on the back. His grin could have reached from Berthold Beitz to the Moon.

*

After Frederik had caught them in the act, Peter Hubbard returned to his small allocation. He was more than a little red in the face.

He did feel oddly liberated, however, perhaps even a little blasé; while he was sure his friend would 'keep mum', he found he wasn't bothered if Jenn or the professor, or anyone else for that matter, learned of his errant liaison with Raquel Sveistrup. Perhaps this was the beginning of a more satisfying partnering for them both, having been to hells and back?

Who knows? But it'll be good to spend time with her, away from the tools. I owe it to myself to have a little fun, right? Why not! Hey – tomorrow's Sunday, our scheduled rest day! That'll give us a chance to grab a few moments…should be interesting, to say the least!

The universe seemed a brighter place. Suddenly, Peter didn't mind his dull, cramped allocation at all now. He smiled at the courtesan's twist in his stomach, the stir in his loin.

There was a small container the size of a clenched fist on his workspace, from today's automated delivery. Its lid was fastened invitingly, with a piece of gold ribbon. Picking it up his heart skipped a beat; the attached greeting was in Jenn's handwriting.

Jenn, oh...oh shit. So she's finally got in touch, the heartless bitch. Thought she might placate me with some gift, or whatever this thing is? I can't breathe, my chest aches. But can I be doing with this, really? I can still feel Raquel tingling on my fingertips. I'd rather be with her right now, if I'm honest.

He considered tossing the red container to one side, but curiosity got the better of him. He untied the gold ribbon and opened it; inside was a small black box with a large red button, intimating it be pressed.

Which of course, he blindly did.

Peter winced as his dormant, temporal link suddenly became active. A pulse from the box cleared a long-forgotten path straight into his mind, instantaneously triggering his immerser's curse. A direct-send lanced painfully through the surgically-implanted device, erupting in unwanted imagery overlaying his visual cortex. He fell to his bunk, hands clamped to his temples, gasping and moaning in agony.

The image was fuzzy, indistinct. Peter tried to fight this techno-pathic intrusion, but the more he resisted, the more it seemed to hurt.

What the – why the hells would that bloody woman send me a message like this? Is it malfunctioning? Maybe it's not from her...I don't care, whatever, I just need it to stop!

He grabbed the black box and stabbed the red button repeatedly, but it was no good.

The imagery settled, became sharper. An all-pervading sense of the sea, a realer-than-real experience of a great briny swell, trampled all his senses. Crashing sounds permeated his mind, his consciousness. The waves hit him, he could taste it, smell it, feel it, the deep blue rising all around… but he found he could articulate some *meaning* from it, too.

Who are you, what do you want, why are you doing this?

He didn't have to actually express the words, not verbally. His very thought processes were inextricably *linked,* to those of this 'sea'.

In great detail, a scene was laid out before him. That evening, as part of the daily haul, an autotug was scheduled to return to Berthold Beitz with a 'ComSat09', for service and repair. He *experienced* images of the beat-up old satellite, to be lashed to a bulkhead in the facility's expansive hangar. With an unreal clarity he suddenly understood all there was to know about the ageing, hunk of space hardware.

There was something precious held in its crystalline memory core, which must be retrieved and returned safely to Earth, at all costs. That's where he came in. He was expected to prise the memory unit free with his bare hands, if he had to.

Right now. Before the next shift started, and crews began their overhaul.

Arrangements had been made for him to then leave, with the corpse of Malik Nayyar, in an autotug. Via Clarke, he was to board an Earth-bound vessel departing 06:00, and the final leg of his transfer would return him to London Galactic via stratotranscender. There he would be met, and would hand over the memory core.

Screw this.

In his immersive state, subversion rose within Peter; a profane counter-attack poured out of him.

Why in the hells should I do this? Who are you? You can go screw yourself, whoever you are!

But the sea responded with a menacing swell. Peter comprehended 'they' had Jenn. They had taken her, they would hurt her in ways he could not possibly imagine, unless he did precisely what he was told. Images of her, hurt and bloody, rolled over him in waves and, in his intoxicated state, Peter emitted a pathetic moan.

The images became hallucinogenic; it was as if he himself was punching her, he could feel her bones shattering beneath his fists. He landed such a blow as to pierce her flesh, but kept going until he grasped her heart. He wrenched it from her twitching body, and squeezed, watching juices run down his arm.

This is what will happen if you disobey.

I'll kill you! All of you! I'll strangle your scrawny necks! Gods, if I ever get my hands on you! I will go to the authorities, the most powerful AI will scour your brains! You won't know suffering like it!

But pain lanced his stomach; his guts twisted in an agonising, nerve-induced intestoration that systematically dismantled his resistance. He doubled over, gasping in shock, in agony, and it wasn't stopping. Not knowing what else to do, Peter quickly submitted.

He would have to perform this task, see it through to the very end. Clearly there was no other choice.

When he returned to London with the memory core, he would be taken to Jenn, and they would both be freed. A reminder of her plight flashed before him, again he was flooded with impressions of her bruised and mutilated, but now he was tearing her bloody face away with his own hands, revealing her skull underneath.

Enough!

He wailed helplessly at the sight; the onslaught pounded what was left of his anger into the ground; all he wanted was to stop her suffering, he would do anything at that point to make it stop.

Intestoration set in, again. The sea rose like a wall, shimmered and glowered as the pain hacked through his stomach. It reached such a height, Peter thought he'd pass out, become consumed by the towering waves. He was reduced to a whimpering child, begging for it to stop.

The great swell pulled away from him at an astonishing rate, taking the intestoration with it. He experienced a curious sensation of falling. A warming wind blew, carrying soothing strokes as he submitted, and the more he gave in, the better it seemed to feel.

With a final, dominating wave, the sea faded from his view. Eventually Peter's real-world vision returned to him.

But the link was still active, like a bee eternally lancing with its sting, at his temple.

Rocking back and forth on his bunk, holding his stomach and head, Peter was left squinting at the bulkhead of his allocation. Sweat trickled down his face from the ordeal.

Who the hells are they? What's happening to me? Where's Jenn?

But these aberrant thoughts triggered horrific intestoration, which again only ebbed when he consciously submitted.

A sensation in his hand caught his attention, he hadn't realised he was still clutching the black box. It crumbled away, reduced to ultra-fine grains of dust by voracious, self-destructing nanos. No trace of it ever having existed.

Head pounding, a reminder of the 'task' leapt to the front of his mind. He would have to go EVA, that was certain, and his heart cowered at the prospect. He recalled the plan hammered into his mind during the assault, details of how he should handle the task, and be back in London safely with Jenn again.

Minutiae clicked instantaneously into place. Auto-suggestive 'immersive-programming' now cut a pathway in his thought processes.

He had no time to waste. Peter emerged from his allocation, holding a hand to his throbbing temple, and hurried off. He bounced off bulkheads and hatchways, before forcing some measure of calm. He got a foot on the ladder up to the carousel, but a slender hand grasped his elbow.

Turning, he saw that it was Raquel.

"Hey there, uh, are you okay?" She seemed unsettled as well. "I'm sorry about what happened earlier, of all the dumb luck, eh? But maybe we can still –"

Her face became serious as she saw his distress.

"Gods, Peter, what is it? What's wrong?"

"Raquel, I-I can't say."

"It's about earlier, right? Freddi's okay, he won't –"

"No, no, it's not that. I-I've got to do something…a task. I –" He winced as intestoration returned, willing him onwards. "I'm sorry, Raquel, I have to go."

"Peter, you seem unwell. What's happened to you? Here, let me get you to sickbay."

He doubled over, and she had to steady him.

"Peter, you're not moving an inch, until you tell me what the hells is going on."

Panting, he told her what he could. As the immersive programming asserted its influence, he could barely gasp most of it, but Raquel was quite adept at piecing the scenario together.

"And this comsat is on board now, in the hangar?"

He nodded, holding his stomach, rubbing his temple.

She hauled him upright. "You'll kill yourself if you go in there, you know that, don't you? You haven't the first idea what you're doing. Why would they want you to do it, anyway? Why not just blackmail one of the hangar crew instead, or me, or even Freddi? We're in and out of there all the time, it's routine for us."

"I don't know. I suppose using auto-suggestive programming would guarantee obedience, that way their plan would be followed to the letter. This would have taken a long time to develop, to nurture in a person," he banged his temple, "they – whoever 'they' are – are in this for the long haul. They must have planted this seed in my mind a long time ago, for it to have this effect on me. That message just formed a trigger, to activate their programme."

"Isn't that sort of thing against the law?"

"You bet your life it is. They're acting above any immersive regulations I know of, that's for sure."

"Gods, Peter, that's terrible. Shouldn't we tell Freddi, get the authorities involved?"

"NO!" He screamed involuntarily. It felt like his stomach was about to burst.

Raquel was incredulous, but when she saw the state he was in, she too realised he truly had no other option.

"Okay, Okay. Here, let me help you, then. From the sounds of it you haven't got much time, right? I'll go out there and get that damned memory core myself then, it'll be quicker if I do it for you. At least you won't get killed in the process."

He let out a painful yelp as the programming asserted itself again. "No, Raquel, it has to be me."

"Well, there's nothing stopping me going out there *with* you though, is there?" She paused for a beat and he didn't scream again. "No? Right, let's get suited up and get you out there, then."

They clambered out through the carousel, and down the central stem to the hangar. She quickly disabled the zone sensors again, and presently they were in the prep area, hefting envirosuits from lockers. They both stripped.

The deck leading to the airlock was criss-crossed with a magnetic grid, so their boots clung to it, giving a little welcome orientation. Quickly, Raquel helped him don the rest of the suit, going over and over EVA protocols and speed-checks, most of which he'd forgotten since his expedited training, which now seemed so long ago.

Suited up herself, she quickly covered their in-built thruster capabilities and lashed standard tool-belts about their waists. She tapped a command and concertina'd visors snapped forward, forming their helmets. The 'blank' envirosuits morphed to hug their figures, and seals stiffened as they trudged heavily towards the airlock.

"Don't gulp air, Peter," she warned in response to his sharp gasping. "Remember what they told you; breathe normally, otherwise you'll hyperventilate. As if we haven't enough problems as it is."

Peter nodded gravely in the confines of his visor. He couldn't stop apologising for what he was putting her through.

She tutted. "Look, just shut up, will you? We'll get you through this, then figure out the next step, okay?"

They stooped into the narrowing chamber, and Raquel closed the pressure door behind them. She skipped the safety checks and began cycling the airlock.

"That's odd," she murmured under her breath, Peter's suit's radio barely catching it.

"What, what is it?"

She gestured the airlock's infopanel. "It seems the airlock's been used once already, this evening." Her shrug was barely evident through her envirosuit. "Recently, too. Your comsat would've been guided in by AI. So I can't think of why anyone would need to be out here, during their rest period. Apart from, of course, an auto-suggestive lunatic, and his equally-crazed collaborator. Naturally."

He tried to smirk, but it hurt too much. Peter hoped silently nobody else would be out here, with them.

Has Volkel escaped his confines and is now on the prowl, baying for my blood? How would he know we'd be here, anyway? Far fetched, but it's possible…

Peter's simmering anxiety went up a few more notches.

"Ah, I know what it is." Raquel nodded knowingly. "It's probably a sensor-ghost from that diagnostic I ran, earlier. When we, uh…you know."

She smiled at him. He attempted a smile back.

Eventually the pressures – or lack thereof – equalised, and the airlock eased silently open, in the vacuum.

"Fine, stick close to me, Peter." She grabbed his arm and they emerged. "Let's get this over with."

Not wanting to draw any unwanted attention from the facility's control space, Raquel had left the hangar lights off. Only the glow from a few infopanels and other equipment offered meagre illumination of the cavernous hangar. She flicked on her suit's headlight, and gestured to Peter to do the same.

Floating some four metres from the mouth of the airlock now, they both scanned the interior, their powerful searchlights slicing great shafts into the darkness.

"That's it there, Raquel."

"You recognise it?"

"Yes, they made me 'see' it in that immersive assault. I know everything there is to know about the bloody thing." Peter's beam fixed on to the chunk of space hardware the size of a bunk, lashed to a bulkhead, its solar arrays stowed.

"She's a biggie." Raquel nudged them in that direction, thumbing her suit's thruster controls. "And an oldie, too. Must have been out here some time, from the look of that damage she's sustained. Too beat up to service in-situ, so she was hauled in. There's less to go wrong if you're inside like this; tools and gear work better at more constant temperatures. Panels housing super-secret memory cores are easier to prise open, if the weather is sunnier, and in general all the more agreeable."

Peter scanned the length of ComSat09 looking for the panel they'd have to remove to access the crystalline memory core. He noticed something was amiss. "Hold on a minute, the panel's already half open. Could it be someone's out here, already?" He panicked, literally throwing them into a spin.

Raquel cursed as she used controlled bursts of her suit's thrusters to correct them, but before she could pull them both away to rethink, another suited figure was suddenly upon them.

Peter turned and illuminated the intruder fully as they rose into view, the visor obscured on their dull-orange envirosuit. Peter failed to react in time as their attacker struck Raquel in the stomach with a large wrench, winding her, and then crashed several times at her visor.

Air was released in a silent, icy out-spray, causing her to tumble away.

Peter looked on in horror as the intruder came after him.

"Raquel!" Peter reached out for her. "Raquel, are you there? Answer me!"

Gods, Volkel has escaped – he must be pretty wild to have attacked the object of his desires like that, he's more homicidal now than ever!

Peter squirmed away, trying to orient his suit's headlamp in the dark chamber.

Where is she now? She was right next to me a second ago! Damn this bloody place, nothing behaves normally out here. Did she reseal her suit?

He could feel blind panic setting in.

Calm, calm. She's professional. She can handle herself in this environment. She'll be back at the airlock by now, you'll see.

Volkel lashed out at Peter but missed, causing himself to spin uncontrollably. Peter wasted several seconds just gawping before trying to plant a blow himself, but he went spinning in the opposite plane. Unskilfully, he activated his suit's thrusters and sped away, bouncing painfully to rest behind another chunk of space hardware, lashed to the opposite bulkhead.

Peter gritted his teeth and had the presence of mind to switch off his suit's headlight. In the dark, he fumbled deeper into the hangar recesses.

"Raquel! Raquel, are you there? Raquel!" He tried repeatedly, but she just wasn't responding. He closed his eyes, fumbled his way into immersion, but his still-activated link failed to locate her presence anywhere; she wasn't connected to any pathway he could see, either to or from the facility's AI.

Volkel must be roaming close now, he could almost *feel* his cloaked presence.

Peter felt sickened to think Volkel could be only metres away! He felt frustrated his organic senses were so useless in this silent darkness. But he had one last thing to try; a long shot granted, but at this point, his options had become severely limited.

My moleware. I can use it on Volkel.

Semi-immersed, he connected with the PAD around his wrist.

He peeked out from behind his hiding place and glimpsed Volkel's silhouette, almost upon him. Forcing his ineffectual eyes closed again, returning to his virtual environment, Peter drew the mole from his PAD like a trail of shimmering gold dust.

The program swirled in his hand. Angrily, he threw it at Volkel, watching it burst and then become absorbed into the very fabric of his 'suit, in a virtual way.

That one's for Mal, you homicidal bastard!

Volkel flinched and writhed, but because of his momentum he kept on coming. With a desperate shove, Peter deflected him off the hulking hardware that had been his refuge, and Volkel bounced back towards the middle sections of the huge hangar.

With the mole now infecting Volkel's suit systems deeply, Peter switched his attacker's thrusters to a diagnostic test cycle. Every thruster nozzle came to life and began pulsating in a regular pattern, causing him to jerk and spin out of control. Quickly, he was flailing about wildly.

Volkel bounced off bulkheads and various space hardware, and Peter saw him grasping at his left arm, evidently in much pain. Knowing he would eventually regain control of his suit, or his thruster fuel would become spent, Peter closed his eyes again and with an immersive direct-send he 'told' the hangar doors to open.

They drew apart silently below, revealing the deep blackness of Earth's night-time shadow, freckled with glowing cities and towns.

Volkel continued to careen around the hangar interior, desperately trying to regain control of his suit's systems, but inevitably his trajectory drew him closer and closer to open space. In a final last-ditch attempt, he reached out for the hangar doors but only proceeded to injure his left arm further as he bounced off the hard frame, and went cart-wheeling into open space.

Volkel span and writhed, but it was useless as his infected systems drew him further and further away from Berthold Beitz.

Auto-suggestive programming drove him on; there was a loose-end for Peter to tie up, that could compromise him!

Bringing his attention back to the now, he closed the doors and quickly sought out Raquel, his heart climbing up through his throat. There she was! He pulled her to him, clumsily, repeatedly calling out to her.

But the toughened polymer bubble of her suit's visor had shattered, was half missing. His headlight revealed her death mask frozen in the vacuum, gasping, contorted into what seemed like the worst death imaginable.

He held her. He stared at her frigid blue face, his mouth opening as wide as hers in horror, and he shook.

No. No this can't be! It simply can't. She shouldn't have even been here with me, in the first place! No, I'm not having it. Let's do this again.

The realisation this tragedy could not be undone by some wave of a magic immersive wand hit him like a sledgehammer. His head pounded.

Intestoration focused his attention.

There was nothing he could do for her, he knew that now. He hadn't even noticed they'd both been tumbling, and only when they were finally at rest did he move them back to the spot he'd found earlier, his temporary refuge when evading Volkel.

It would still be many hours before the next shift started, but he still couldn't allow her to be found too quickly, and have the alarm raised while he was still anywhere near the facility. Frederik Diter would alert the authorities and his escaping autotug would be grounded, putting Jenn in jeopardy as well; therefore dear Raquel's sacrifice would have been utterly for nothing.

With deep reverence, taking care not to injure this poor woman further, Peter took his time and gritted his teeth against the searing lance in his stomach. Tenderly he lashed her there, to rest. He stroked her face, hands trembling, his suit's gloves conveying much of the tactile contact.

"You feel so cold. Gods, Raquel, I'm so, so sorry. You were right. We really have no business being out her, we're just not ready for this life. We're really not."

His instruction asserted itself and, with robot-like detachment, Peter returned his attention to retrieving ComSat09's crystalline memory core.

Thankfully he found it was still aboard the satellite; evidently Volkel had not been able to get hold of it before he and Raquel had disturbed him.

*

The rest of the task, and the transfer back to Earth, was a prolonged endurance test, the likes of which Peter Hubbard had never known.

He cried for Raquel, sweet Raquel...his heart pounded for Jenn, although he couldn't quite pin down *why*.

In the murky darkness of the autotug, folded into a small space next to Malik's bodybag, he'd plugged into emergency provisions, to maintain his suit's systems. He spent the transfer to Clarke just holding tight, wishing he'd worn a proper diaper.

Am I anxious to see her released? Or do I just want to see this through, so Raquel's death wasn't in vain? Oh, Raquel...

He stared at the silhouette of his assistant, lashed to the bulkhead.

I feel nothing for him, still. Why?

Any other time, he would have been languishing in a self-indulgent stupor by now, but his immersive-programming kept bringing him back into line.

The immerser's curse just wasn't letting up. He would have given anything to ease back his visor to rub his temple, even just a little. But the thought set his stomach knotting. He wished he could score some soothes, he needed them badly right now.

The culprits behind the immersive assault had really done a job on him. And it was beginning to dawn on him just who that was.

He couldn't escape the sea; he felt its presence, eternal, lurking in the shallows of his subconscious. It was always *there.*

I remember that image so clearly, from before. On Earth, back at AeroDomont. It was him.

Professor Gerard Moray. His mentor had used impressions of the sea on his work space mood-wall to intimidate and overwhelm Peter. When he'd effectively decreed he take on this test mission, in the first place.

Sure, effort had been put in to making the techno-pathic assault anonymous, but the arrogant old fool just couldn't resist steamrollering me with his favourite mode of intimidation, could he? To flatten my resistance, good and proper.

It all started to make a little more sense now, to Peter's beleaguered mind.

All that, so I could be out here, at this precise moment, to retrieve this?

He nursed the egg-shaped memory core burning a hole in his thigh pocket.

But he didn't bank on Volkel nearly screwing it all up, did he? And taking out dear Raquel in the process. And as for Mal...how could he have screwed that up so badly as well? Sending him out here in the state he was in. Was he really that expendable?

His assistant's bodybag looked misshapen, inhuman, as though there really wasn't a person inside there at all.

And as for Marla...I suppose I can get Summer to check-in on her, if I get a chance. But how did Moray know ComSat09 was going to be picked up, at that precise moment? What does this memory core contain? What does he want with it?

Peter felt queasy as the autotug's retros fired, in a long series of decelerating pulses.

We must be about to dock at Clarke. I hope they're not too surprised to find me in here, with Mal. What am I going to say to them?

After much inelegant jarring and one final, muffled *jolt,* pressures equalised with a rising hiss. The hatchway sprung open and Peter grimaced as piercing light poured in. The solitary cargo handler stayed silent as he unclipped Mal, and heaved them both out of the autotug.

His assistant was passed down the accessway, and bobbing in micro-g, Peter was led to a small cubicle where it was suggested he clean himself up, and get changed.

When he emerged a moment later, the cargo handler gestured at Peter's PAD, pointed at the arrow over the hatchway indicating departures and swiftly disappeared.

Peter frowned for a moment, then understood. Rubbing his temple, he propelled himself along the accessway, then through the hatchway as gracefully as he could.

The return craft to Earth was a stratotranscender; Peter caught a glimpse of the sleek vessel through the gate viewport, as he was ushered aboard with the other passengers. Security was strict, medical checks thorough, AI analysed. His immersive-programming kept his facial muscles, posture, body temperature, even his pupil dilation, within unremarkable parameters.

122

The return trip was slow, and cramped.

When the stratotranscender did eventually hit atmosphere, lulling boredom was replaced instantly by high anxiety, despite soothing announcements from the cabin crew. They tried their best to reassure passengers that the violent flames licking at each viewport, and the bone-jarring shaking, were all perfectly normal.

Peter gritted his teeth, and endured re-entry.

Why in the hells would anybody put themselves through such a wretched experience voluntarily? That's it, right here and now I'm making a personal pledge to never again venture from Earth's sweet cradle.

The flight arrived somewhat late, there had been a security alert at London Galactic. But finally, Peter was moving through the disembarkation lounge. He felt heavier; mother Earth's gravity clawed at his aching frame. His head pounded with every footfall, and he thought he might throw up.

What if word has reached here from Berthold Beitz? What if I'm arrested for Raquel's murder? Or has the professor seen to it that I pass through here, as well?

He was ushered through quickly enough, by a thoroughly disinterested border official.

The size, the onslaught of the arrivals lounge battered his senses. He stopped and looked about, wondering what to do next, and got caught up in the bustling throng pushing past him. He walked the length of joyous faces celebrating returning loved ones, but he couldn't see if any were for him.

A figure materialised from behind; evidently male, his carewear bland, anonymous. They took a firm grasp of his arm and led him towards one of the quieter corner exits, where a small autopod sat waiting.

"I've got the memory core!" Peter didn't try to hide his desperation. "Where is she? You told me she would be safe. Are you going to take me to her now? What have you done with her?"

The figure ignored his repeated pleas. He was shown to the rear passenger door, it was intimated he should get in. Peter felt under no illusion he had any real choice in the matter. The door slid closed, and locked behind him. The figure got into the front passenger compartment, joining a second figure who was equally anonymous.

"Where are you taking me?" Peter wondered if they could hear him through the Plexiglas divide separating them. He sat back, rubbing worriedly at the crystalline memory core now clenched in his fist.

After several miles of autoway cruising, the first figure turned to regard Peter, their lean face dispassionate.

Peter sat forward, his jaw slack, wordlessly waiting to see what would happen next.

The separating divide powered down, and suddenly there was a look of intensity on their face, a fire in their eyes.

Before Peter could react, he felt a blinding flash of white-pain, a stab from within his link again, but this time far more intense and concentrated.

He blacked out instantly, slumping back into the seat.

*

LONDON

Professor Gerard Moray had to bring his immersive session to a close more quickly than his ageing faculties would ordinarily permit. In fact, his head swam, and he felt queasy.

By all accounts, the operation was now an autopod wreck. The opportunity of seizing the sought-after Huldrych data had eluded him, his man had been compromised. And in the process, he'd managed to arouse the attention of the omnipotent Bureau09, as well. He'd thoroughly blown it.

Foremost in his mind now was, therefore, self-preservation.

This had been somewhat of a last-chance scenario, and his masters would not reward him well for this latest failure. Especially not for letting the promising Hubbard-asset slip through his fingers, to be delivered straight into their opponents' hands. He'd played the long game, had gambled much on his protégé; oh, the plans he'd had for him…but it just wasn't to be.

A myriad of scenarios coursed through his mind. Sombrely, Moray reached the conclusion that, because of this debacle, he must now disappear. Assuming he wanted to go on sucking oxygen.

Transcending mere alternate-IDs and quaint cover-names, he already had the engines firing on his own contingency plan. A series of meticulous manoeuvres that would eventually see him disappear quite effectively, if he held his nerve and properly executed each phase. For he had the means to do so, having secretly turned his previous assignment ('last year's fiasco', they'd called it) to his financial advantage.

But right now, he must act with great haste.

Starting at what was left of Mauritius, he would perform a sequence of globe-trotting steps to waylay pursuant operatives, until he could reach his final destination. Conservative estimates had it taking years, possibly as many as ten, before his departure would finally bear fruit. But Moray was confident he would eventually see out his remaining days on Luna, as per his plan.

At AeroDomont, effecting his escape mere moments before company agents burst into his workspace, Professor Gerard Moray was gone.

ORDEAL

EARTH

The striking blow winded Peter Hubbard. He writhed in the chair, his arms and his ankles tied.

The seat was rickety, it swayed under him. His head hurt really badly, he couldn't see a thing, but he vaguely felt something against his face. Was he hooded? His nose didn't feel right either, he couldn't breathe through it.

Everything tasted of metal. The right side of his jaw ached, terribly.

He sucked air finally through his mouth, his diaphragm extending in a reflex action. His breathing came in great gulps.

"Who is your controller?" The voice was not so far away; it sounded Nordic.

Peter sobbed. "I don't know what a controller is." His mouth didn't feel right. Had he lost some teeth? "I work for AeroDomont, in Lon –"

Another blow to his gut, not winding him this time, but definitely hurting him.

A pause. Silence broken by Peter gasping lungfuls of air, again.

"Who is your controller?" The Nordic voice, much closer this time.

"I don't know what one of those is. Could you mean my boss, Professor Moray?"

Silence. There were low murmurings in a language Peter couldn't understand, but respite was all too brief before another blow, to the gut. Then another, although somewhat off-centre as it landed too far up, and right. The bottom two of Peter's ribs on that side cracked.

He yelped, wanting to clutch his side but, bound thoroughly to the chair, he just swayed again. Some movement, and low murmuring again. Then another blow, followed by the same question.

After what seemed like an eternity, Peter could barely mumble his responses, let alone talk.

A bell rang, a screech to Peter's wretched senses.

A hollow plastic *clack,* and the voice was mumbling softly.

"Shouldn't take long, he's soft. He's close to breaking already… yes. Yes, I will."

Nobody answered. That hollow *clack* again.

Peter was roughly untied from the chair; he felt a sensation of rope around his wrists, as they were re-tied behind his back. Still hooded, he was pulled to his feet, but he collapsed immediately to the ground in a heap.

He was dragged for several metres. He was thrown, but felt the comfort of a bare, old fashioned mattress beneath him. A metal clunk at what must have been an even older bedstead, banging against an adjacent wall.

He was rolled over on to his good side, and a rough pair of hands probed his cracked ribs; they stopped prodding when he screamed. Something was strapped to his right arm; he felt a curious scratching sensation before being filled with a *charge* that emanated from the area, a strange feeling of energy being literally pumped into him.

Brights.

Peter wanted to sleep. He wanted to nurse his sore head, hold his hand against his broken ribs, even rub his stinging wrists and ankles, but he couldn't. The brights rejuvenated, re-energised, and he trembled; there was no way he would be getting any rest.

His tormentors were keeping him awake, between bouts of physical torture and that same question, over and over again.

"Who is your controller?"

They'd started on his face – he'd endured several sessions of being punched and beaten. Then it had been his gut.

For what, four sessions in a row? Then it was my groin... felt like they were planting a boot. I still can't feel anything down there. Then my fingernails. Then it was my face again, or had that been before they went for my groin? The most recent stuff has definitely been all about my trunk though, right?

He'd lost track.

He'd begged, pleaded with them from the start; why were they doing this? Where was Jenn, was she safe? What did they want? Every time he'd mentioned her name, though, something hard struck him on the bridge of his nose, so he'd quickly learned to refrain from mentioning her again.

How's long's this been going on for, now? Almost a week? I can't take it, I'm going insane. Where's Jenn? No! Don't even think of her!

Peter lost all track of time; his ordeal had, in fact, been going on for a little under two days.

My nose must be well broken by now, gods! No wonder I can't breathe through it.

He'd surpassed the state of total despair, retreating into numbness, where gallows humour was his sole companion.

Hmmm, my leg feels warm – ahhh...must be pissing myself again.

He was dragged off the bed, and it started over.

Who is your controller? Thump!

Who is your controller? Thwack!

Who is your controller? Crack!

Peter lost consciousness several times during that particular session, and towards the end he reverted to a baser state. He mumbled pleas for them to let him die.

He was allowed a break. Peter Hubbard just sat, breathing badly.

Then it all recommenced.

The relentless questioning, the beatings, this time a return of the boot to the groinal region. But Peter found he couldn't answer any of their questions, even if he could speak. Nothing worked on him any more. He now just wanted to die.

Eventually, it ceased. They dragged him away, no longer of any use, and on the urine-soaked mattress he was allowed to succumb to the sweet release of unconsciousness.

They had thoroughly broken him.

*

Coming to, Peter found that, while his wrists and ankles were still bound, his ribs had been bandaged. A sharp, painful trickle of air was able to pass through his nose. He didn't have the sensation of something over his face any more; his eyes rolled sluggishly about.

He shivered at the cold.

He thought he could see a pencil-thin line of bright light, but he couldn't be sure as the world would just not stop spinning. His eyes wouldn't stay open properly. He closed them, welcoming the darkness.

Several moments passed, and he wasn't accosted by his torturers.

His senses slowly returned, like lights coming on in an allocation, but to his peril. His wretched body was in a state beyond perpetual pain, his head ached so much from abuse and fatigue. He began to moan, he was one with despair. Facing an insurmountable cliff erupting before him, his mind responded and lapsed him into unconsciousness again.

Time passed.

Noise awoke Peter. He jerked, then clenched his eyes at the sudden onrush of painful, white light. He could see the red shapes in his eyelids, and stared in wonder at them. His attention was lost as his mind lapsed again towards a dream-like state.

Yelling, more crashing from wherever the light was coming from.

He jerked again. Gingerly, he parted his eyes; he was in a small cell it seemed, and the light came bursting through the door as it came crashing open.

A figure stepped in and wrenched open his clothing, before stomping off again. They returned with a hosepipe, to wash him down. Peter writhed and squirmed but the figure was quite thorough, meticulous in reaching every part of his wretched body, with the icy-cold blast.

Dripping, shivering, Peter was dragged out of the cell and tied roughly to the same rickety chair. Tentatively, he opened his eyes as best he could, but found that wasn't very far at all. At least, not as far as he remembered they could open. His eyes rolled around, bewildered.

No blows to the balls, no questions. Not yet anyway.

The figure appeared to his right, and scratched his arm with something. Peter winced, feeling an icy chill spread throughout his body that made the hosepipe seem like a hot spring.

He whimpered, as the frigid tentacles of the injection reached his neck, his head, and permeated his very mind. From within his brain he had a contradictory impression; scouring heat despite the icy cold, like a pathway was being cleared, burnt away. He cried for them to stop; he wanted to hold his head.

After a while the agony started to ebb, but then his other arm was injected. The torment started again, a little more on his left side, this time. Peter clenched what was left of his teeth, the colossal pain that *was* his jaw proving a temporary distraction from the hellish ice scorching clean his synaptic pathways.

The intense pain abruptly ceased. Peter was hugely grateful to the figure still bearing down on him, for not scratching his arm and frying his brain with ice again.

Another presence came closer, a smaller man perhaps, and pulled his aching head from left to right, and then shone a pencil-thin beam of pure excruciation into each eye.

The small man murmured, some Nordic language. Peter recognised the voice of his interrogator. He wanted to reach out and hold him, *show* him he was no threat, that he would do whatever he wanted, only please make it stop.

"Don't worry." The small man patted Peter on the face, making him moan. "You're just about ready, now."

The other figure to Peter's right untied him from the chair, and dragged him back to the cell. Tossed on to the cold, soaking mattress, Peter was rebound and injected again. Squirming in anticipation of the effects, Peter soon calmed as the most welcome, warming sensation coursed through his veins. It brought with it a sense of *nourishment,* and a little pain relief.

Through exhaustion and plain old submission, Peter Hubbard went blissfully under again.

*

Voices woke Peter. Groggily, he opened his eyes. Two figures were standing just outside the doorway to the cell, one small, one beefier. Again, they were conversing in that language he just didn't understand.

He blinked woozily, tried to focus. Beefier seemed to notice he was awake, and stepped in.

Peter whimpered, tried to recoil within himself.

Beefier rolled Peter to one side, evidently checking to see if he'd soiled himself again. Satisfied he hadn't, he pulled him off the metal bed and dragged him, moaning, back out into that bright room again.

The rope wasn't so tight this time, but nonetheless Peter was retied to the rickety chair. Able to open one of his eyes a little more, he could finally take in some of his surroundings, albeit in fuzzy double-vision.

The chair was wooden, and so was the bare floor. The small man was seated behind a wooden table, arms folded, studying him. But Peter paid him no mind as his dubious senses wandered around the room again; wood-panelled walls, a slanting wooden roof, what looked like an old-fashioned telephone, mounted on the wall to his left.

Through the pungent, metallic taste in his sinuses, Peter thought he could smell fish mixed with effluence.

I suppose that must be me, then.

"So…" Small's voice came softly from behind the wooden table. He had a cruel face, the kind that enjoyed inflicting suffering. Peter thought he noticed a buff folder open containing pieces of actual *paper*, but he couldn't be sure. "Peter Michael Billington Hubbard. Born Blackburn, Lancashire, United Kingdom. Moved to Richmond, UK, aged three years, after the death of both parents. Studied Engineering at Imperial College, graduated with a First after completing a placement at CalTech, before returning to graduate with a Masters under sponsorship of AeroDomont, no less."

He nodded in appreciation of Peter's résumé, then looked him in the eye. "Who is your controller?"

Fleetingly, Peter wanted to ask about Jenn, but he buckled quickly at the thought of what they'd do to his nose. He worked his jaw, coughed and spluttered a few times, until he could murmur again.

"I-I'm sorry but I still don't know what one of those is, I'm afraid…" he braced himself as Beefier approached and lamped him one on the side of the face, the side that wasn't already badly swollen.

"Who is your controller?"

Peter didn't respond, and had another blow across the face, to thank him for his reticence.

132

Silence as Small stood from behind the wooden table, and came round the front. He sat upon its edge, arms folded, regarding him solemnly.

"How long have you known Moray?" He was almost conversational now. Beefier moved a little, making Peter cower.

"Ummm...since my placement year, at uni."

I hope he can understand what I'm saying, through my broken face. I don't want to get struck again. I've got to make the effort to speak more clearly!

"When did he first approach you?"

"Ummm...when I was researching my thesis, at Caltech."

"What day was it? What time of the day?"

"Ummm...I don't remember."

Beefier stirred again.

"I-I think it was afternoon time," Peter spoke quickly, anything to keep him at bay. "I'm not sure of the day. I-I think it was a Thursday."

"What was the date?"

"Ummm...I don't recall, honestly." Peter moaned and writhed in reaction to the blows that hadn't even come yet.

"What time of year was it? How long had you been there?"

"After the Christmas break, must have been when the January term started...would have been sometime in the second week, yes."

"Where did he approach you, which room at Caltech?"

"Ummm...in the student library, his aide said he wanted to see me, umm…in his office."

"And where was his office?"

"In the newer block."

"What number was on the door?"

"Ummm…B07, I think."

"What colour were the walls?"

"White."

"How much furniture did he have?"

"Just a workspace, and chair."

"What did you sit on, then?"

"I sat on a spare seat."

"Oh, so there were two chairs, then?"

"Ummm…"

Beefier gave him a right-hander, for that one.

"Well, was there or wasn't there?"

"I –"

Beefier stepped forward and belted him again. The questioning resumed thick and fast, and Peter did a bad job of keeping up. "Who was the aide that approached you, what was their name? What did they look like? Did they work on campus, or had they come over to the Americas with Moray?"

The line of questioning and beatings went on, and on. Peter had to recall virtually every detail of that first meeting with the professor, even down to how Moray had been dressed, and who else may have been around at the time. Only when every last morsel of detail had been revealed, did the same line of questioning start all over again.

Beefier approached Peter, and he squirmed and moaned, whimpering at the thought of what was to come.

Small raised a placating hand. "It's okay, Peter, this will make you feel better."

Another scratch to the arm but this time, a curious sensation of *excitement* spread throughout Peter's body, and the pain and tension that'd been his waking life just *melted* away. Peter felt affable, open, like he genuinely wanted to please his captors.

"So, tell me. How long have you known Moray? When did he first approach you? What colour was his office, at Caltech?"

Peter lost count of the number of times they went through the same loop of enquiry, but thanks to that last injection, he didn't mind at all.

Not one bit…this is great!

Each time he was asked a specific question, he felt compelled – he *needed* – to give the most truthful answer he could. And every time the same question came around, he was able to include even more detail, as he dredged his memory.

The beatings became less frequent, and Peter was allowed to drink water from a chipped metal mug with a free, albeit trembling, hand. He was given some fishy broth that burned his lips and made him heave, but at last he was getting sustenance.

And the same line of questioning resumed.

Peter was allowed to sleep for what seemed like luxurious lengths of time. Awoken for the next sessions, he would be secured to the wooden chair in the wooden room, with Small behind the wooden table, and Beefier increasingly in the periphery. And then began the same line of enquiry all over again, dissecting Peter's story under a microscope, scouring each morsel for irregularities.

He would then be drugged, that curious sensation to speak the truth, the whole truth, and nothing but the truth would return…and the questions would start all over again.

"How long have you known Moray?"

This went on for several more sessions, and he was beaten when his answers inevitably turned churlish, insolent. After the latest round, Peter was left shivering on the metal bed in his cell as usual, but this time the door had been left wide open.

Laying there, he stared at the slanted, bright doorway, and fought back unconsciousness, just for a moment.

For the first time since his detainment, he heard a haunting melody, something carried along by the frigid air that stroked him like a soft feather. A piano sonata that had a familiar ring to it, something he couldn't quite put his finger on.

The steady tempo and rolling melody comforted Peter. Its simple elegance stroked his beleaguered soul, and the rising crescendo gave him hope.

Peter was given a clean pair of faded, denim coveralls, a blanket, water jug, and a chamber pot. He was 'encouraged' to use some of the freezing cold water to wash himself, before each session.

He was allowed a free hand during his questioning, to feed himself from the roiling bowl of thick, fishy broth that would sit steaming on his lap, burning his legs, and the crust of bread. But Peter was grateful for the warmth, any warmth. He found he could just about chew the bread if he left it in the broth, to soak.

"Tell me how you came to join AeroDomont." From behind the wooden table, Small never tired. Beefier was circling.

"Moray offered me my first placement, a solid-status position that came with a two-space allocation, all my own. I'd have the opportunity to work with some of the finest minds in the industry, he said. On the bleeding edge of R&D.

"I was encouraged to develop my working theories into practical models, then prototypes. Eventually I was given an assistant, Malik Nayyar, who was also new to the company. Together, we developed my DZ prototype, it went better than expected. Mal had a sharp mind. Such a shame…"

"Focus."

"Yes. So we knew we were on the right track. The professor was happy with our progress. One could almost say he was impressed."

"Describe how you came to meet your girlfriend."

"Pardon me?" Peter squirmed and glanced at Beefier, who was drawing closer. His nose ached in anticipation of blows, at the mention of her.

Small gestured Beefier to back off. "It's okay. Tell me how you met."

Words did not exactly flow. But Peter's heart surged at the thought of her, his 'life'. "It was a chance meeting, really. In main reception space, at AeroDomont. I was heading in, as usual. It had been raining, and I looked a mess. She said I must remember to bring an umbrella next time; to be honest I didn't know what to say back to her. But she introduced herself, and asked who I was.

"So I told her. What I did, my position there. My status seemed to impress her. In fact, we were on our first date the following evening."

"Who asked who out?"

"Um, let me see…well, she said she'd like to get to know me. And I thought it would impress her if I asked her out, to a Somalounge they'd just opened. Over where my allocation was, at the time. Um…is she okay?"

Small let the insolence slide. "What day of the week was it when she picked you up? What was the date? What exact time of day was it?"

Peter did the best he could, scouring his memory for details. They didn't inject him with the truth serum this time, nor mete out persuasive beatings.

"…so that's when Mal and I first assembled a beta-version of my Deazy. The board were so impressed I got my double allocation, and she moved in shortly afterwards."

"Okay." Small sat back in his seat. "Go through it all, again."

Over several more sessions, Peter's responses became automatic. His cooperation was rewarded with more food, and an extra blanket was left for him, in his cell. Then the line of enquiry progressed to how he'd been posted to Berthold Beitz. Peter recalled the curious behaviours exhibited by both the professor and Jenn, during the run-up to his trip out there.

He recounted the work with the Deazy, his relationship with Raquel Sveistrup, Malik's passing. Then the 'task' given to him by Moray, and the run-in with Raquel's assistant Hans Volkel in the hangar – resulting in both their deaths – before returning to Earth, with the memory core safely in his keep.

Peter slept, he had no idea how long for, but he welcomed the escape slumber brought. Awoken some hours later, he was encouraged to wash himself, and was given a fresh pair of equally worn blue coveralls.

A little more gently this time he was pulled out of the cell, to be faced with Small sat again behind the wooden table. Peter's eyes could open some more now. For the first time, he noticed how his interrogator was dressed; black shoes, black trousers and a black roll-neck sweater contrasting severely with his pale, cruel face.

"Get yourself settled."

Small waved away the bonds about to be applied by Beefier.

Peter was given something to eat. He trembled because of the cool air, despite the warm meal on his lap.

"It's time to make an introduction. You can call me O'Neill. You have been cooperative, you're getting rewards. But if you don't mind, there are a few details I'd like to go over again."

O'Neill studied him from behind the wooden table, his cold eyes scrutinising.

"So, Peter Billington-Hubbard, let's start from the very beginning. How long have you known Professor Gerard Moray?"

EARTH

Peter Hubbard felt he was being slowly settled into a day/night-time routine.

When he wasn't being ceaselessly questioned by O'Neill covering the same ground over and over, he was allowed to eat and rest. His face felt swollen, his mouth still hurt mightily whenever he ate or spoke, but his ribs were on the mend and he was able to stand unsupported for longer periods of time.

Encouraged to exercise, he began by gingerly pacing the length of his cell, before collapsing in exhaustion on to the bed. But over time, two cell-lengths became four, which became six, and so on until he could easily make ten. He also found if he turned the bedstead up against the filthy wall, he could make a more circular route.

Push-ups were an agonising ordeal. His atrophied muscles protested, but his fingers thrummed more, in crippling agony.

I vaguely remember fingernail torture…they must've broken one or two of them, as well. Best be careful, don't want to make them any worse.

Stomach crunches were slow in coming, cracked ribs stabbing white pain into his very brain. However, Beefier was unrelenting in his 'encouragement' and, eventually, Peter was able to perform regular sets of each.

How long have I been here? Where in fact is 'here'? Why are they doing this? What's happened to Jenn?

Peter kept these inner musings at the back of his mind – his nose still ached in anticipation of the punishment he would surely receive, should he ask out loud. But on occasion he would allow himself to ponder, as he waited for sleep to arrive. All the while, that mysterious piano sonata echoed into his cell.

Slowly, gradually, Peter's strength was allowed to build.

Sessions on the wooden chair were marked by a significant change, though it took Peter a while to notice; Beefier was no longer anywhere to be seen, it was just him and O'Neill. It did cross his mind to get up and run for it, but he was utterly beaten.

Peter worked his stiff, swollen jaw as he stared away from his interrogator, answering the never-ending slew of questions.

O'Neill reclined in his seat and regarded him, his skeletal face a dispassionate, oily mask. He glanced down at the open buff folder on the wooden table and closed it, a symbolic gesture it seemed, for he was about to move Peter on, to the next stage.

"Cold?"

Peter nodded. He crossed both arms, and hugged himself as best he could, busted ribs notwithstanding.

"Perhaps it's time for me to introduce you to Franklin, then." O'Neill gestured at the doorway and Peter looked up wearily. Rising to his feet he steadied himself on the rickety wooden chair, and followed O'Neill into the next room.

The wall of heat felt marvellous, the onrush of cooking and spices tantalised his senses. And coffee? It was a kitchen, quite sparse and utilitarian as per the rest of the quarters. Something very furry was curled up in the corner; perhaps it was a pet? The animal seemed to pay them no heed, so Peter guessed he should ignore it as well.

Daylight. Perhaps it was late evening? The low-glow from the square windows illuminated the kitchen without the need of the harsh electric lighting of the interrogation room. Peter glimpsed a scrubby farmyard, with a large red barn, outside.

He could hear livestock, the cries of – what were they, sheep?

O'Neill gestured Peter to sit on another wooden chair, only this one had quilted padding on the seat, and back. Peter welcomed the comfort. Heat emanated from a hideous, metal monstrosity with a bulbous flue reaching into the ceiling. O'Neill fussed by the outside door and returned with some wood, which he fed into the stove with a gloved hand.

He hefted a glass bottle filled with some thick looking white liquid, and as it clinked against the ring on his finger the furry animal roused at the familiar sound. Although household pets had become less commonplace, Peter knew a cat when he saw one. The fat furry creature trotted over to O'Neill and watched expectantly as he poured a saucer of the white liquid, before consuming it hungrily.

Peter watched fascinated as O'Neill grabbed two chipped metal mugs and returned to the stove, setting to work brewing a concoction in an archaic black pan. He poured two mugsful of the rich-smelling brown liquid and offered one to Peter, sitting next to him. "The finest kakao in the world. Just like Mother used to make."

Peter sipped carefully at the hot chocolate.

"Better than the rubbish you get from an automat, eh?"

Peter nodded and tried not to gag on the richness of the drink, but enjoyed the warmth. Slowly, his taste buds made the adjustment.

"Allow me to introduce you to Franklin, our stove. He heats the whole place, you know. We even figured out a way of harnessing the excess heat to run the lights." He took a long draw of his kakao, and clapped his lips apart with a satisfied *mwahhhh*...

Peter was startled and almost dropped his kakao as the fat, hairy cat leapt on to his lap, having evidently finished its meal. At first Peter didn't know what to do and the animal just sat there, licking its lips and staring. So he tried patting its fur with his free hand, and that seemed to do the trick. The cat closed its eyes and purred.

"Ah yes, that is Breidr. Our domesticated forest cat. He's been with us here for a long time, now. We found him as a kitten. It took patience and lots of scratches before he accepted us. Forest cats are usually quite svelte creatures, but since he joined us, the domestic life seems to have suited itself to him."

The thing weighed a tonne. Peter wanted to shoo it off his lap, but he dared not through fear of reprisals. Eventually, though, O'Neill hefted it back on to the floor, and the cat curled up at his feet. Then he leant in, too closely to Peter. "I just want you to know you're doing a good job, Peter; you're progressing well."

Peter daren't look him in the eye.

"And if you continue to give us what we want, things will carry on getting better for you. I've already introduced you to Franklin, a *full six* days before AI predicted you'd be ready," he went on, his eyes taking on a cold sheen, like those of a child pulling the legs off a spider, "but I broke you quite quickly. Well…*relatively* quickly. I now sense you're ready to move on. Get us out of that dusty old interrogation room, eh? Maybe see a little daylight." O'Neill sneered as he gestured the small windows, with his half-empty mug of kakao.

Peter sat, stilted, feeling like he had a loaded gun against his head.

O'Neill settled again and regarded Franklin, their stove. "Of course, if you fail to give me what I want, I'll have to tear off your toenails and beat your balls between two bricks."

Peter's trembling hand causing his kakao to splash a little.

"Good…" O'Neill sounded thoroughly pleased with himself. "Looks like you're even softer than we thought. I don't need to fiddle with your new temporal implant yet, to control your baser instincts. That shows you're adapting well; you should be pleased. We took out your expensive surgically grafted link, by the way. Just in case you've been wondering." O'Neill tapped his own temple, with a knowing wink.

Peter hunched with gritted teeth, bracing himself for whatever was coming next.

O'Neill placed a placating hand on his arm, his tone was soft. "So, Peter, tell me. How long have you known Professor Gerard Moray?"

Peter blew out a huge lungful of air. He hadn't realised he'd been holding his breath.

*

Peter was permitted supervised access to the kitchen, at regular intervals. He got more of a natural grip on the day/night cycle, around him. After what he supposed had been three or four more days of cosy chats with O'Neill, Franklin, and the snoozing Breidr, he was taken outdoors, on to the farm proper.

He blinked in the daylight, and couldn't look directly 'up'. The sky was a white sheet of cloud that hurt his eyes

Gods, the grass seems so green, after that bland interior.

He felt exposed, vulnerable, cold. Quite conditioned, he remained still. He said and did absolutely nothing, until he was told to.

Beefier reappeared on the scene, and had brought a thick jumper for Peter to wear underneath his faded denim coveralls. From an era pre-dating carewear, the bulky garment felt rough and itchy.

O'Neill stirred behind him, as he dressed. "That's authentic lambs' wool, you know. A rarity, where you come from. And although that pullover's old now, I bet it'd be worth more than you made last year, and then some."

Peter supposed it was late afternoon; the Sun was low and it was quite fresh. Breidr had sensibly stayed indoors, presumably curled within the range of Franklin.

Peter had a curious sensation of being 'at altitude'. He caught a glimpse of a mountain range and open water, several kilometres downhill to the left. Security was obviously his captors' thing, a high fence ringed the farmyard, easily two square kilometres, maybe more. Besides the big red barn, there were a number of pens and enclosures, for livestock.

Gods, it stinks here – and what are those? Actual live chickens, pecking around? And are those pigs over there…and sheep?

Peter risked a glance over his shoulder, and caught a glimpse of their wooden quarters. It surprised him how relatively small it was.

143

So the boarded up windows must my 'cell', and the 'interrogation room'. Cosy.

A large ground vehicle was parked on the other side of the quarters, but not an autopod, something bigger and more basic. No doubt the primary means of getting on and off this farm.

Beefier appeared from behind and gripped Peter's arm tightly, causing a weak yowl. He was marched over to the pig pens. Peter screwed his nose up at the snuffling, noisy animals and felt instant revulsion.

"Get in." Beefier shoved Peter against the wooden fencing. He climbed nervously in, transfixed by his new company, and quite convinced one of them was about to eat him.

Are pigs carnivorous? I've no idea, I've never even seen one before. Not in the flesh, as it were, and certainly not as close as this.

He stood whimpering, holding his hands at chest height, but the swine were completely disinterested in his presence. Unless of course he planned on feeding them.

Beefier threw Peter a shovel, and he looked at it dumbly. The man gestured at the large container at the corner of the pen, and told Peter to start shovelling shit.

Peter really had little choice; it was either that or have his balls set between two bricks, as O'Neill had so delicately put it. Not doing a very good job at hiding his utter disgust, Peter shovelled the first load of excrement, and immediately vomited. Knowing there would be no let-up, he shovelled his own puke along with the next load of pig shit, while still retching.

After Peter had completed his arduous task, he tried to stand erect, but his back wouldn't have it. His legs trembled under the strain, and it looked as though he would drop at any moment.

"Get him back inside," O'Neill told Beefier, "but wash him down first. I don't want the Sjøhus smelling of that shit."

The following morning Peter found himself shovelling pig shit again, while fighting to retain his breakfast. O'Neill watched carefully.

When Peter had moved the last shovel-load, O'Neill announced they would be having pork for lunch today.

Exhausted and bewildered, Peter stood there propped up by the shovel. Beefier handed him a large, flat knife. He looked up at O'Neill, totally missing the point they were trying to make.

After almost ten seconds staring incredulously back at Peter, O'Neill barked, "Slaughter one of the pigs, you idiot."

Peter looked down at the blissfully ignorant animals, wondering what in the solar system he should do.

Flat-out refusal will be met with an inevitably excruciating rebuttal...my biggest problem is how to actually kill a pig, with a knife? At this point it's irrelevant whether I should, or I shouldn't.

After Peter's interminable prevarication, O'Neill bellowed. "DO IT!"

Peter flinched and his knife-hand shook. Fearful of reprisals he chose a target and just 'plunged' with the blade. The pig kicked and squealed away from him, the knife still protruding from its back. Peter attempted to chase after the wounded animal while slipping in the mud and bounding off the other denizens of the pen, who were evidently annoyed their routine had been so rudely disrupted.

"No, that's not how you do it!" O'Neill was aghast at what he was witnessing.

Peter looked over at him helplessly, at this point covered from head to toe in muck.

"Go on, show him," O'Neill ordered Beefier, who climbed into the pen and quickly cornered the injured animal. He held the unfortunate beast between his legs, virtually sitting on the wretched thing.

He yanked the knife free and handed it calmly back to Peter. He made a 'throat slashing' gesture, and held on to the squirming beast.

Gods, no, I can't believe this...

Peter gulped, and his hands shook even more. But at least he had more of an idea of what to do, now. He crouched just off to one side of the animal, and tried slashing at its throat.

That didn't work.

The first couple of attempts merely yielded superficial cuts, causing the pig to thrash about even more. So Peter tried a sawing action, but slipped with the blade and almost took his own eye out.

Beefier, struggling to keep the shrieking animal under control, hissed into his ear. "Deeply, and *upwards*!"

Wow, that breath! Does this guy brush with rotting meat?

Peter swallowed and tried again. This time his stroke was strong and true, releasing a large shower of claret, spurting everywhere. The unfortunate pig squealed and cried as its time came to an end, and Beefier didn't let go until the thrashing eventually stopped. A couple of the other pigs looked on but, in the main, the other animals in the drove were quite content to continue about their business.

Peter fell to one side, panting, badly shaken by the ordeal. He was covered quite thoroughly in a cacky blend of mud, blood and pig shit.

O'Neill commanded from his vantage point. "Next time, you do it on your own. Now bring that bloody thing over to the Sjøhus, the house. The job's not finished yet."

That day they ate chops, and breakfasted on bacon for a week.

*

Peter continued to work the farm.

O'Neill explained that the farm buildings were ex-'Rorbuer' fishermen's cabins, modernised some time ago to incorporate the larger 'Sjøhus'. Unfamiliar with these terms and hesitant to ask, Peter just nodded.

While it seemed the harvesting of pig shit remained his domain exclusively, as his strength grew Peter was allowed to help tend the sheep, as well. He felt muscle mass returning and his stamina

146

building; the work outdoors was rejuvenating him. His broken face was covered in beard, now. It itched almost as badly as his jumper. His hair felt quite long, too.

I can't remember when I last saw my own reflection. Not sure if I'd want to...

He would spend most evenings going back over his life story with O'Neill, in the company of Breidr and Franklin, with kakao in hand. During one of these evening sessions, O'Neill introduced Peter to his hulking, antique 'Parlophone' sat in the corner. The wooden object was more like a piece of furniture than anything else, and very carefully he drew a large, flat-square object from one of its flanking shelves.

"This, you will find, is called a 'CD'." O'Neill slid a large, black disc out of the cardboard sleeve. "A rare object, from hundreds of years ago. It stands for 'Compakt Diskette'. Antiquated by today's standards, of course. I've no idea how data was re-written into these curious grooves. Perhaps they were write-once. I could dig deeper into the topic, but there's more allure in some things remaining a mystery."

He placed it on to the Parlophone, as a mother would lay her newborn down to rest. He activated the hulking device with a plasticky *click,* and the disc began to spin. O'Neill then gently applied a pivoting arm culminating in a tiny, protruding needle that scratched along the surface of his 'CD'.

Slightly muffled, scratchy music emanated from the body of the curious setup.

"This is my favourite CD, out of my whole collection. My particular favourite 'track' is called the 'Adagio Cantabile'. I play it every night."

They sat in silence enjoying the seven-minute opening, the 'Grave', before moving on to the second movement.

Before the first note had even finished, Peter recognised the haunting sonata that caressed him off to sleep each night. He glanced quickly at the CD's curious cardboard 'sleeve', to identify the composer.

"Beethoven, yes," O'Neill purred, "he was one of the founders of classical music. A pianist at the age of three, I believe. Wrote over forty symphonies, married into French royalty. Remarkable."

Peter felt himself relax a little, as the purring, lap-mounted Breidr pressed his sitting bones deeper into the seat. For the first time for as long as he could remember, he actually felt himself beginning to let go.

8

CONSPIRACIES

NORWAY

Under supervision, Peter Hubbard was allowed to walk the farm perimeter, whenever he wasn't sleeping, eating or shovelling shit.

One morning, Beefier had appeared and set more of a 'pace'. A shuffling stroll became a fast-walk, then a jog. Quickly, Peter has collapsed to the floor, his chest heaving.

Gods, my teeth itch. My mouth feels so thick – I can't spit hard enough. Don't think I've run like that since my schooldays!

Hauled to his feet, Peter was 'encouraged' to jog some more. By the end of the week, he was building his cardio-vascular recovery rates, and on day ten he found he could jog for nearly fifteen minutes, without being totally wiped out.

During the runs, his thoughts were clearing, becoming lucid. Also, he became more aware of the parts of his body that hurt, and those that didn't.

Certainly, his jaw felt tight, like somebody had replaced it with a hunk of mahogany. His nose felt 'thick', although he could breathe through it rather well, now. Broken ribs were mostly A-OK. His fingertips were still bound-up, he wasn't sure how far his nails would have grown back by now, after their removal during the interrogation. But the pain emanating from the link on his left temple, the immerser's curse…that just wasn't going away.

Thoughts of Jenn, of Raquel, kept popping to the surface. Through fear of reprisal (not to mention those two bricks versus his testicles), Peter used the challenge of exercise to repress his innermost thoughts and feelings. Especially as he wondered what was in that mysterious red barn, every time he jogged past it.

O'Neill joined him when his routine was less strenuous, and the relentless questioning took on a different flavour. O'Neill slowly switched from merciless probing to more 'sounding out' of his understanding of the Geo-Political systems making up the world of today.

Peter related cautiously his understanding. "There are three main power blocks. The United States of the Americas, the Pan-Asian Alliance, and what's left of Europa-State."

"Go on."

"Um…there's the all-pervading corporate dominance, of course. Influencing and shaping state policy. But we live in an increasingly free world."

O'Neill tutted, shook his head.

Gods, have I said something wrong? I'm fearing the double-brick treatment, now.

"And there it is. That typical air of apathy; a conscious, blissful ignorance that's way too prevalent in the modern populace, today. I ought to beat your balls especially for that. Lazy compliance, casual disinterest in the way things are done, giving the collective a more bovine mentality than anything else.

"Sure, it's old-hat to control a population through fear. Tools like disease, stratotranscenders crashing, autopod accidents, food and housing shortages, climate disasters. This fight against 'radicalised terror' the puppet media ram down people's throats, with such hysterical frenzy…it's all manipulation, all a means of control. They'll let a maniac attach himself to a cause and blow up schools, if it suits their agenda before taking him out. But the puppetry runs far deeper than most realise.

"The high black-arts of 'steering the herd' are so sophisticated now, it takes surprisingly little for AI to sway the masses. All it takes is a pandemic here, a 'revolutionary' new concept there, and *bang*. The science of control has become so refined, as long as they have their automats, their manufactariums, their immersive links, people couldn't care less if some crazy presents 'the truth' to them. Even on a silver platter. It's all too soon ridiculed into obscurity, because they're told to. Or worse; simply ignored.

"But total domination takes a number of forms, most especially through immersive suggestion. Control in its purest form doesn't just mean dictating what a person says or does, it means steering their very *thought processes,* as well. Whoever got there first with the temporal link hit the bullseye; you can manipulate the herd's general way of thinking beautifully, with those things. And they don't even know it's being done to them. It's like handing the levers of your brain over to a complete stranger, and trusting them completely. Brilliant.

"What does escape them, and the muzzled puppet media, is the relentless cold war raging between the big three. Forget patriotism, forget territory – wherever it may be in the Solar System. It's about a level of control no system can fully conceptualise, no end state that can ever be totally satisfied, and certainly no end goal any corporate-state can ever permanently attain. Imagine it's sort of like a constant one-upmanship; nobody knows who started it, nobody can actually win it, yet none of the competing factions ever dares to back down, through fear of being swept away by the other.

"And it's impossible, even for the architects of it all, to untangle the complex web of subterfuge that now spans our Solar System. In fact, more often than not, the means are so convoluted, so *impenetrable,* the opposing factions in a particular incident may ultimately report to the *same* masters anyway, at the end of the day. So what's the point of it all, eh?

"But you've got to stay primed, keep 'em on their toes, right? And these silent, dehumanising battles are being fought right under everybody's noses. It's just that the main populace choose not to notice.

"On the surface, we're all seen to be working together, for the greater good. *'Astra Domi Nostrae',* and all that. But of course, you've had a dose of the *reality* yourself, now. The states can't just rely on prolific technology any more, to get what they want. They need to fully exploit their *organic* resources as well – the people. Those expected to devote not only their lives to the untenable cause, but unwittingly offer their very *souls* as well. You're an example of this. There have been many like you. And, believe me, there will be plenty more, after you."

O'Neill stopped, and looked Peter in the eye. "You know that memory core they told you to get, from that old satellite? Its data had deteriorated to beyond useless, yet still it cost lives to appropriate. Just look at what it's cost you, personally. And all for nothing. That's the level things have reduced to."

Peter's frown deepened considerably. He looked down at his feet. If he could have felt his jaw, it would have tightened.

"Yes, that's right," O'Neill sneered, "you went through that whole ordeal, lost everything, because a small bounty was suddenly on the market. And powerful people wanted it. All of that, for what only amounted to a few engine schematics anyway – a couple of months' head start in the race for the next 'space engine', that would take us to Mars and back in half the bloody time."

Peter's chest heaved.

O'Neill shrugged. "But you know what? Ours is not to reason why."

I can't believe what I'm hearing. My life's ruined, gods know what has happened to Jenn, Raquel's dead, I killed Volkel...I've lost so much. All that for the sake of some something that was unusable, anyway? Gods, I think I might throw up...

His chest tightened in anger.

O'Neill nodded. "And so the penny drops. Unfair, isn't it? You want to tear somebody's eyeballs out, right? This is the *real* world we live in. But it was more than just a case of wrong place/wrong time, for you. You were groomed for this, since he picked you up. That's why you were recruited, by Moray. So he could have an asset like you in his back pocket, and manoeuvre you into position when he needed to.

"No doubt he had other, bigger things in mind for you, after this all played out. But it all went a bit wrong for him, didn't it? We got to you first. Actually, you were the classic sleeper agent, even *you* didn't know what was going on. All that was needed from him was a manipulation here, a threat to your status there, and *voilà*. Your prototype was an ironclad cover to place an operative, to have you out there more or less the same time that old satellite would get picked up.

"I have to admit, you and that woman caught our man completely by surprise, when you blundered into that hangar. The way you went about dealing with him too was, uh...unique. That moleware thing of yours is a really neat idea; that's what got me thinking there may be some potential in you, after all. If you're capable of designing something like that, we'd snap up those kinds of skills. Anyway, back to the point...so you were plucked at the perfect age, and groomed by Moray.

"It would've all been carefully choreographed, your status at AeroDomont, your allocation...Even 'Jenn'. I'd say she was put there to keep tabs on you, to push when needed. Quite obvious really, when you look back. But, like the rest of his operation, we didn't spot her, either."

O'Neill paused, while Peter absorbed that last nugget of information.

Jenn was a part of it? Kept tabs, pushed when needed...no way, he doesn't know her the way I do. That's not how it was, at all!

O'Neill raised an eyebrow.

It can't be! I want to laugh, surely it must be some mistake... Jenn and I were – are – in love!

Shock seized Peter, as he realised the truth of it.

As if a million-piece jigsaw puzzle just fell into place...her coldness, her distance. Then all over me in an animalistic frenzy... how she manoeuvred me so well, into accepting the test mission. Gods...the humiliation.

A tear rolled down his cheek, and he dabbed at it quickly through fear of reprisal. But his captor merely placed a placating hand on his shoulder.

"She's still alive, as best we can tell. She put up one hell of a fight, though, during the tussle for the data. She took a hefty beating from our operative, before it got uploaded to that old satellite. Then she went to ground. But we understand she's resurfaced on another *Oma* assignment. Similar to the one she was on, with you."

Peter couldn't control his outburst. It was as though the final brick of life's sanctity had been wrenched away, and the wall came tumbling down on top of him. He was a hollow husk, he had nothing now. He fell to his knees, sobbing.

Very quickly, Beefier appeared. O'Neill watched Peter for several moments, moaning on the cold ground in the foetal position. He signalled to the other man.

Beefier carried him back to the Sjøhus, to his cell. There, Peter Hubbard was allowed to spend the remainder of the afternoon alone, with his grief.

*

The crackle of wood inside Franklin was harsh, in the modest-sized kitchen.

Peter Hubbard just stared at the orange flames, dancing and leaping behind the grille. Late, it was dark outside. Apart from the fire, the only other source of illumination was the electric lighting, spilling in from the adjacent interrogation room. Peter stroked absently at Breider's soft fur; the cat was curled in his lap.

O'Neill put on the Parlophone, and the air was gradually filled with the subtle nuances of the *Pathétique*. He poured Peter another kakao from the large simmering pan. Silently, Peter nursed the old, chipped white metal mug, and held on to it as if it was the last thing in the world he possessed – which in fact, wasn't far from the truth.

154

Peter's eyes were a washed-out hazel, his face an impassive mask. His life was gone, his whole world torn apart; certainly, the last period with Jenn and the professor had all been a house of cards, blown down by the tiniest breath.

How am I to ever recover from that? What have I got now?

He could hardly go back 'home', back to his 'life' at AeroDomont. He thought of his late assistant Malik Nayyar, he thought of Marla, of their loss.

O'Neill cleared his throat. "It took some doing, you know, holding them off and allowing me to bring you here. For re-education. There were colleagues who would've taken a pair of pliers and a screwdriver to you, for what you did. But I held them off, told them I saw the potential in you. Those were quite the breakthroughs you'd made, that moleware and your 'Deazy' thing. The skills behind them are what keep you alive.

"We're affiliated with Europa Space Liaison – our niche is Bureau09, although we tend to operate with a great deal of autonomy. Our members are many, and diverse. Some are deployed in more offensive positions than others, some planted in sleeper cells, awaiting activation. Some mole operatives exist, deep under cover. And that's all you'll ever need to know about your new masters.

"Because, the way I see it, you don't have much choice but to accept you're ours. Either that, or we hand you over to the authorities, for what's-her-name's murder. Or we could feed you to your beloved pigs, one chunk at a time."

O'Neill's eyes bore into him. Peter gazed at his nearly depleted kakao.

Focus. Ah look, not much choco left…still, the last mouthfuls are always the best, the richest. They're my favourite.

"Yeah, that's what I thought. Of course, you'll receive a new identity. We'll get you over to the operating room in the morning; you must've been wondering what's in the big red barn, outside?

Amongst other things, we've a well-equipped operating theatre, for plastic surgery and, well...should a guest in our keep need serious medical attention, in the process of their re-education.

"Let's see now...I'd say we need to thicken your brow a bit, slim down your jawline, raise your ears a little, that's all. Nothing too drastic. It'll be painful, but it'll be effective – and lasting. We'll leave your nose the way it's healed naturally, all broad and flat like that. The temporal link we fitted you with, that's there to stay. Can't go back to you having a surgically implanted one, can we? You'll stick out a mile, in the kind of work we have planned for you."

O'Neill lapsed into a thoughtful silence. Peter's stomach churned, and his mind reeled in despair.

What the hells is happening to me? What kind of 'work' is he talking about?

Mechanically, he continued to stroke Breidr's soft fur, the animal snoozing contentedly on his lap.

"I have the perfect identity for you to take on, one of my better IDs. I've been cultivating it for years. 'Legends', they used to call them. Back in the olden days. 'Marc Devin' is who you'll become. He's got a technical background like yourself, a Brit, similar build, dark like you, bit of a loner...shouldn't be too difficult to manage, especially once you've learned his legend inside and out. We'll tune your link, to properly mesh with your brain. Then, we can keep proper tabs on you. Intestoration will be your guide."

Peter shifted uneasily, as his stomach churned in memory of the excruciating means of exerting control.

"We'll set you up as technician, with UniTech. Everybody contracts with them, meaning we'll be able to place you practically anywhere, anytime. Any installation out there that suits our needs. Maybe you'll watch a person of interest, or take them out. Switch a circuit board for a substitute, or blow-up another. Or even just steal something for us, before the other side gets there first. Like Claudette did, with that memory core.

"But we'll need to toughen you up some more. We'll sow that essential, killer-instinct into you, just so you don't grow flabby and useless on us…" O'Neill leant over and quickly hurled the sleeping Breidr against Franklin, and threw his empty mug against the metal stove with an almighty clatter. The scolded, shrieking cat turned and hissed at him.

Peter twisted in his chair, steeling himself.

What the hells?!

"You see?" O'Neill reclined, making himself comfortable again. "Even though he's grown soft and fat on us, our dear Breidr still has that instinct for survival, that basic compulsion to fight back. And that's what we'll breed into you, *Devin*."

Peter – Marc Devin – tore his eyes from O'Neill's, and stared back at the fire.

Then my life is truly lost. How can I ever escape this? What in the hells will they have me doing; will I have to go back out there, into space again? No! How can I dodge this, and live to tell the tale? A future as some zero-status grease monkey, grubbing around in the filthy underbelly of space colonisation…useful only in carrying out this Bureau's dirty work, only to be discarded again.

His eyes lost focus as he stared at the contained inferno, behind Franklin's grille.

Peter Hubbard was dead.

Long live Marc Devin!

9

DEVIN

NORWAY

Surgery was a gruelling experience. They had only bothered with absolutely minimal, local anaesthetic; O'Neill had made the observation it would do his pain threshold the world of good.

They didn't bother to wait for the wounds to heal either, before tuning his temporal link. They had to strap him to that rickety chair, though, because probing his mind turned out to be particularly agonising. It took an immersive-assault to form pathways, in programming the neuro-linguistics of the Devin legend. The problem had been his lack of any real previous immersive activity; the task was akin to hacking a jungle clearing using only a blunt knife. They literally burned the new personality traits into his mind, to better interface with his link.

Dumped into his cell, he wasn't given pain relief, but the Marc Devin dossier to study. He was told he would be tested, in the morning. Scanning the old-fashioned paper documentation that night, he found it evoked ghost-like memories of him having lived the events, on the page. Immersive programming at its finest. Whenever his concentration waned, whenever he lost focus and just wanted to give up, nerve-induced intestoration returned.

The engineer that was inside Devin understood the science behind it.

It's all electrical, the relationship between mind and body. Tap this through a link, and crippling pain, or exquisite pleasure, can be triggered with just ones and zeros. By stimulating the gut's pain receptors, they think I'll eventually unlearn my old habits by aversion, and develop new ones, as a result. Marc Devin's traits come to the fore, thus 'Peter Hubbard' becomes a distant memory. And godsdammit, it seems to be working…

It only took a few days. Tied to the rickety chair again, he was hooded and interrogated anew, but this time testing his integration of the Marc Devin legend. Eventually his answers became so fluid and confident, the conscious volitions of who had been Peter Hubbard, meshed seamlessly with those of the encroaching Marc Devin personality.

Finally sat before Franklin, O'Neill had expressed his satisfaction with this case.

"If only they'd all go as smoothly as this, I'd be a warmer human being. But here," he said as he reached down beside him, "as a symbolic gesture, I want you to deal with these." He handed Devin the last personal effects of Peter Hubbard – his ID, his PAD – and gestured at Franklin.

Devin rolled the two artefacts around in his hands before standing, opening Franklin's grille, and tossing them in.

O'Neill made a contented noise. "Tomorrow, we'll move on to your next phase of training. Call it 'survival-spycraft', if you will. We'll have to expedite things a little, though, as I don't want to miss out on an opportunity that's come about for your first proper assignment."

Marc Devin gulped.

Deep down, his guts tightened, his link combining morbid fear with intestoration.

*

Devin was taught to withstand interrogation, if picked up. He learned how to handle a weapon, to shoot. How to surveil, how to 'vanish'. How to evade, to kill.

Slaughtering pigs was one thing, but they slammed into him the knowledge, the skill, to do it for real. To people. He was taught about encoding routines, a special language of hand gestures, murmurs he could use, should he think he was being listened to.

He was taught how to lie convincingly, the science of persuasion. How to cover his tracks, to spot probing questions and dodge malicious, immersive attacks. How to look like he meant one thing, while the whole time doing the complete opposite.

He was taught a great deal about human nature. How he could use universal traits found in most people in today's society, to his advantage. He learned a lot about assessing, very quickly, whether or not somebody was a threat.

For the first time since his arrival, he was allowed to leave the confines of the farm, under close supervision, of course. O'Neill didn't need to make clear the consequences, should he try and make a run for it.

The pair clambered aboard the vehicle, parked behind the Sjøhus.

A cool, crisp morning, O'Neill took manual and drove them along the rocky water's edge. Devin enjoyed a palpable sense of freedom, albeit on the end of a very short leash.

All those other autopods are on the wrong side of the road – and so are we. Are those Norwegian markings I can make out?

After thirty minutes' drive, they arrived at a village sign-posted 'Henningsvaer, Lofoten'.

I have absolutely no idea what part of Norway that is.

O'Neill smirked. "You probably wondered why the cold never quits? You're up in the Arctic Circle, that's why. Despite the climate change. Henningsvaer's a fishing village, never known for its sunnier climes."

The archipelago became prominent as they rolled over a soaring, linking bridge, from the mainland. Small buildings grew in clusters, and the road became a patchwork of streets closing in around them, lined with traditional-looking wooden buildings and other Sjøhus structures. There was a smattering of visitors, mixed with the few locals.

O'Neill parked them near the Heimøya church, and they got out of the vehicle.

Never raising his voice above a low murmur, O'Neill pointed out all the behavioural traits and patterns evident even here, in this small cross-section of society. He asked Devin questions on how he might surveil that white building over there, what would be the best way of gaining entry. Also, how he could kill that woman over there, with minimum fuss. Could he manage it unnoticed? What would his exit route be?

They visited a small café, part-filled with tourists. Having been sat for a moment sipping inferior kakao, O'Neill resumed the questioning.

"What colour hat is the woman wearing, behind you?"

"Dark red."

"How many people are sat over by the window; is there anything unusual about them?"

"Six. Four children, two parents. None of them are looking him in the eye. He probably beats them."

What's the optimal exit route, should a member of the opposition burst in right now, and spot you? What's your link telling you about the place, apart from the usual blurb they feed the tourists? Where would the best place be to start a fire, if you wanted to raze the place to the ground?

Devin's gut twisted with intestoration every time he hesitated, or got something wrong. But slowly, O'Neill layered the reprogramming, helping him use his link in ways he'd never thought possible.

That had only been their first field trip, and already Devin's head felt it would burst. After more visits to town they spent each evening going over and over what they had learnt, and the more glaring mistakes Devin had made.

Devin became increasingly competent, at the basics. The roles would frequently switch, where he would be telling O'Neill what he was seeing, what he was judging, what he was sensing, and the potentials within any given situation.

He was allowed to reconnoitre chosen areas alone, and flash encoded reports back to O'Neill via their immersive-link. He got better at conducting basic exchanges of sensitive information in crowded places, using only grunts and gestures. They practised evasion, with Devin given sixty seconds' head start, O'Neill's superior skills and experience, of course, always closing-in. But Devin managed to avoid capture for increasingly longer periods of time.

O'Neill slapped him heartily on the back. "Okay, so I think you're about ready now for your final test."

Devin was sent to Henningsvaer alone, to collect a parcel from the old Postkontor. With his senses now more attuned to anything and everything going on around him, he quickly spotted that he'd grown a tail – a tall, slim man, clean shaven, with glasses, fur hat and a long woollen coat.

He had no immersive presence, at least none that Devin could detect. He did all he could to nullify his own immersive trace as well, gritting his teeth as the ever-present throb in his temple increased.

The night was drawing in early, as it tended to this time of year. Devin stowed the small parcel in his clothing; he instinctively felt returning it intact was also part of the test. Using his link to overlay routes and possibilities before his very eyes, he began his evasion routine.

It seemed as if his tail was deliberately pushing them both deeper, into the village, away from his vehicle.

No doubt a ploy of O'Neill's.

But no matter which way he turned, however many flights of stairs he went up or down, the tail remained. Devin pushed on towards the waterside, where fleets of fishing boats were harboured.

By now, it was quite dark.

Devin headed briskly for one of the small wooden jetties, reaching out on to the water. He knew the tail would be on to him soon, but he quickly doubled back so that, perhaps for once, he would be behind *him*.

The area was quite deserted; he crouched in the darkness behind a wooden support reaching deep into the frigid water, and waited. The creaking of the boardwalk broke the silence, giving the man away. Devin burst out from his hiding place, and was upon him.

Is that a weapon he's holding?

Devin had no time to analyse the situation further; he planted a kick in his stomach, winding him, and slammed him against the wooden support. He let out a muffled yelp as his left side crashed into it, and as he bounced back, Devin spun his leg across the floor, knocking one of the other man's from under him. They staggered, and a final shove caused them to tumble sideways, into the icy water below.

Quickly but quietly, Marc Devin headed directly back towards the village, initially keeping to the shadows, and then moving more freely amongst the few people still out and about. He checked for the tail regularly, and reconnoitred his parked vehicle before approaching.

Only when he was convinced of the all clear did he climb aboard and drive calmly out of Henningsvaer, back to the farm.

*

Marc Devin arrived back in good time, and was met in the kitchen. O'Neill ripped open the parcel and retrieved its contents; another sealed container of the high-quality cocoa powder he needed, for his kakao, and another containing thick, white liquid.

"I'm glad this got through okay. It's so much better than the *stuff* they peddle to the tourists, in Henningsvaer." O'Neill put the pan on for them, and presented a saucer of the white liquid before Breidr.

"Genuine cow's milk. Becoming quite expensive these days. Bovine disease must be on the rise again."

Devin didn't care; he'd gone through all that hassle, just for a better tasting hot chocolate. What satisfied him was that he'd evidently completed his task to the correct standard, even doing so without any intestinal repercussions.

"So. Did you get a good look at your tail, then?"

"I did."

"And…?"

"Quite a tall man. Slim build, clean shaven, looked like he could have originated from Europa-State. Wore those old-style glasses."

O'Neill handed Devin a mug of kakao. Sitting, he looked down at his drink, his face serious. "I see."

O'Neill had Devin explain his evasion routine, and chuckled when he described how he'd finally shaken off his pursuer, by plunging him into the icy waters. They went over and over the details of the evasion, and a number of mistakes were pointed out to him. But whilst it seemed, on the whole, Devin had done quite well, clearly something was amiss.

The door to the outside burst open, startling Breidr. A tall bespectacled figure entered, dressed in a fur hat and long, woollen coat. Still dripping and holding his left side, Devin recognised his pursuer. He stirred in his seat, but O'Neill placed a hand to quickly settle him.

The pursuer entered the kitchen proper, muttering some expletive in German, while painfully removing his sodden coat. He positioned himself in front of Franklin, to warm and dry through. He took off his antique spectacles and began wiping at their lenses ineffectually, with a damp cuff.

Devin froze in his seat as he recognised his pursuer; it was Frederik Diter. What was the Berthold Beitz coordinator doing here? Clean shaven, soaking and more than a little rattled, but it was most definitely him.

"I believe you know Freddi." O'Neill's voice had that edge again. He glared at Devin, as if to say he should have recognised him when he first spotted a tail, beard or not. Devin stewed and felt chided for not seeing Frederik Diter in that face, for summarily dismissing the man's likeness. His guts tightened in anticipation of the reprimand he was sure to receive.

Diter stowed his spectacles and nursed his sore left arm, but that wayward twinkle was back in his eyes. "A good job you most certainly made there, Peter, on me. It was tough to keep up with you in town, but I enjoyed the swim!"

Devin just looked back dumbly, wondering what in the solar system Frederik was doing down here on Earth, in Lofoten.

His link prompted a more logical analysis and, gathering the facts at hand, he came to a few conclusions pretty quickly.

So he's a member of Bureau09 as well then, would've been 'their man' aboard Berthold Beitz...there to retrieve that memory core...Gods, it wasn't Volkel I sent spinning out into free space, it was Freddi! I expect he wants to kill me.

Devin couldn't help enlightenment spread across his face.

Frederik Diter didn't stop staring, a little wild-eyed, at Devin. It didn't help he was soaking wet through. "That is right. A good job you made for me there also, in space. You took me by surprise; I did not imagine there would be other persons in that hangar. And then bam, there you are!"

Diter clapped his hands together, noisily in the confines.

"But there are two of you; Raquel Sveistrup, also. I guess she must make help for you, for sure. It is with regret she dies but that is the nature of our work. As a professional to another, I must say that, and now you will understand. I know you were both two lovers, though I am convinced that is all, between you. It would have been good, to have recruited her for us. *Wie schade.* From the beginning I studied you. Did you know this?"

O'Neill piped up. "Freddi's the best I know at judging people. That's why we're sure even *you* didn't know why you were out there."

"For sure, the opposition made such a good job of you. And for all the problems you have made for me, I would like to make a good job of you, very much!" He burst out laughing, startling Devin. There was something unnerving too, about the way Frederik was eyeing him.

"But, hey, we can still make friendship. We can take that program you hit me with in space, this is good, to use over on our side."

O'Neill nodded. "You'll have it soon enough."

Devin smiled weakly and just nodded. He didn't know what to say.

O'Neill gestured. "Freddi is here to brief you on your first assignment. And, moving forward, he'll be your controller, within the Bureau. Certainly, for the longer term. And regarding your case," he exchanged a glance with Diter, "there's a loose-end we want you to take care of. Balance the books, so to speak."

Frederik Diter nodded and grinned back at Devin, that twinkle back in his eye. Marc Devin gritted his teeth.

*

PARIS

As per instructions, Marc Devin was seated outside a bustling pavement café, in the middle of the *Quatrième Arrondissement*. By now early December, the streets were adorned in all manner of Christmas paraphernalia and medical-masked tourists came and went in their droves. The occasional driverless autopod made sudden stops and detours, in avoiding them.

It was early afternoon, and the Sun was still bright. The air was crisper than when he'd first arrived. As a precautionary measure, Devin placed both hands around his generous-sized cup of chocolat-chaud, to warm them. He'd grown quite accustomed to the stuff, be it Norwegian, French, whatever.

He was watching the small bistro opposite, awaiting the arrival of his target, due any moment now. He had no idea who he or she was, only that his link would chime when he saw her/him. But the target would be here today; he was to confirm the identity, then await further instructions.

Gods, I hope it's Moray. If I could get my hands on that old bastard, what I'd do to him...

His link squirted a chord of recognition as a small, slender woman with black hair, fashionable sunglasses and red coat appeared. She took an outside table, and studied the menu.

Devin had failed to spot Frederik Diter during training in Lofoten. A mistake he would never make again. He studied the lines of the woman's face, her stature, soaking it all in, not missing a detail.

It was Jenn.

Gods, it's my Jenn.

He sat incredulous, trying his best to not let it show. He blinked several times and exploited the capabilities of his link, but whether he liked it or not, it was most definitely her. Ambivalence threatened to overwhelm as he was suddenly awash with a *need* for his lost love, and also the very real desire to hurt her back for what she had done to him. His intestines tightened in an effort to centre his thoughts.

What the hells am I going to do?

His cognition triggered an unlocking in his link; Frederik Diter's words floated to the surface of his mind.

'Kill her.'

He sat motionless for a while, not knowing what to do. Discomfort slowly started to build in his stomach. He tried to ignore the rising intestoration.

Should I go over and confront her?

She was in the same dirty business he now found himself in, but could he just grab her and make a run for it, hope for the best? His stomach knotted at his every subversive thought; the more time he spent not killing her, the worse it got.

But then he remembered how she and Moray had gotten him into this mess, in the first place. How it was her who'd done such a job, manipulating him. He tried to cloak his emotional outpouring from those around him, but it was difficult.

Devin fumbled for a small black box in his pocket, and activated the short-range damping field that would specifically target Jenn. Her ability to direct-send for help was severed and, suddenly sensing this, she looked about her quickly, her guard immediately up.

Devin touched her with a send, and she looked straight over at him. They stared for several seconds as she took stock of the situation. She slid her sunglasses down her nose.

'Peter? Is that you?' she sent back.

'Yes Jenn, it's me.' Neither of their lips moved during the whole immersive exchange. *'Have you missed me?'*

'Peter, I…' Her countenance trailed off, but then in the callous manner he'd so frequently experienced, she hit directly at the point. *'What do you want?'*

This angered Devin.

What do I want? Is she serious?

He let down his cloak a little, and loaded his words with more of his festering emotion, quite literally so she'd *feel* as much as hear each his response. He trembled, not altogether because of the intestoration, though it kicked up another notch.

'You used me, Jenn. You destroyed my life.'

She blinked as she absorbed the full impact of his emotionally loaded send. Then looked back at him with infuriating nonchalance. *'So they've got you as well, eh? You were just another job, Peter. Surely you must understand that. It was nothing personal; no hard feelings?'*

His anger came to boiling point, he needed no direct-send for her to appreciate that.

She looked about herself cautiously, sensing she was being cornered. *'Hey, I'm just a professional, paid to do a job. Just like you are now, right?'*

And then she changed her tack.

'Oh, hey, Peter, baby…It doesn't have to be like this, we can still be together, just you and I. Like old times. I can make you feel good…They don't have to know about it, either. Come on. Let's escape from all this madness, just me and you. I love you, Peter. I truly do.'

This pushed him closer to the edge, and she knew it. It was clear she was just stalling for time until she worked out her exit plan, and still she persisted with the sweet words.

'Let's get away from them, Peter, they shouldn't come between us like this. Our love is forever.'

'Liar!' He offloaded such a blast of emotion, she was taken aback.

'Oh, come on, baby; don't be like that.' She stood from her table and turned her back to him.

Tears rolled down Devin's face as he brought his mind back to his assignment; to kill her. As he got back on track, the enduring intestoration ebbed considerably and, still holding the dampening field on her, he noticed an empty autopod approaching from up the boulevard.

It took effort, but he maintained his link with her, and threw his moleware at the vehicle's guidance systems at the same time.

'Goodbye, Jenn,' he sent, remorsefully.

She glanced round at him quickly, shouldering her handbag. Tourists yelped as they jumped out of the path of the oncoming autopod, apparently out of control as it mounted the pavement. It slammed Jenn and maybe two or three other diners against the glass frontage of the bistro, sending them instantly to their deaths.

The boulevard went into uproar as Devin felt his immersive link with her sever. He loosened his iron grip on the autopod. What had just happened should be impossible, they would say. When the authorities conducted their investigation, they would find no trace whatsoever of his sophisticated mole program in its control systems. Just another computer glitch, one in a million, happens all the time, right?

As the whole place screamed and bodies flew about, Marc Devin remained seated, nursing his chocolat-chaud. Deciding it was finally the right temperature to sup upon, he decanted a shot from the soothe-seller into the brown liquid, and took a long draw. He allowed his link to soften and cajole him, despite the continuing immerser's curse. Finally, his stomach went to rest as it appeared he'd fulfilled his mission parameters.

Better make it look good.

He darted his attention around, and gawped suddenly at the scene, remembering that his demeanour should resemble those around him, or else be registered as anomalous by local AI.

He noted that some of the other diners were still partaking in their meals; evidently, nothing interrupted *le déjeuner*.

So he brought his attention back to his drink. The tears were still there, and his hands still trembled. In his emotional turmoil he focused his attention on to the rich, silky drink as it cascaded down his throat. The luxurious flavour, that deep aroma… he recalled the calming effect the kakao had had on him back in Lofoten. He felt the connection cement itself in his mind. It struck him what a truly majestic drink this most surely was.

His link was making a little headway relaxing him, a reward for a job well done. But, in a whirl, his mind continued to cycle through anguish, horror and despair. So he concentrated on finishing the drink, and felt a rush as his link pepped his taste buds, in compensation. He smiled at the large, ceramic cup and placed it back down on to the table with a measured calm.

His body tingled as a sureness flooded through him. The furore on the other side of the street reached fever point as he linked with the bistro's automat, and paid. He rose, arranging his dull, anonymous clothing in a meticulous manner.

He chewed on a soothe, from the pack in his pocket. He strode off down the boulevard, in the opposite direction to the mayhem he'd created, glancing over his shoulder in concern to make it look good.

Marc Devin wondered idly what they'd have him do for his next assignment.

I, A SPY

10 days later
PARIS

Marc Devin was naked save for a small towel around his waist. Staring out of the hotel window, he watched a stratotranscender lift from Charles de Gaulle Spaceport, and climb steadily into space.

His gut twisted but through no intestoration; come morning, he'd be on one of those craft, hurling 450 souls out there into low Earth orbit.

Where he'd begin his next assignment, for Bureau09.

I can't bear the thought of going back into space. Not after what happened last time. Who the hells actually wants to be out there, anyway?

But they had him; O'Neill, Diter. Despair closed in, like a shroud. But his instinct for survival was strong, too strong still for him to give up all hope. At his wayward thoughts, a brief intestoration was his reward. He bent in agony.

Gods, it hurts. But just another few seconds, nearly through it...

He gasps as it stops, he tended to hold his breath during intestorations.

The magenta sky heralded sunset. Blinking lights made their ascent, the accompanying roar only *just* curtailed by the thick, polymer windows.

The flickering newsfeed he had running from the old infopanel caught his attention again. He preferred this to exacerbating his eternal headache through unnecessary immersion and direct-send.

The ongoing investigation into the cause of the recent autopod disaster, killing four pedestrians, had run its course. Officials could not deny links to Eartherradical terror groups, but announced their investigations would remain ongoing which, essentially, was newspeak for them closing the case. Contracts with the mighty

United States of the Americas' supplier, Goodman Interplanetary, were under review, and autopod manufacture was rumoured to be switching to a Europa-State base.

As collateral, that's at least one free shot I've made, at one of the Bureau's main opponents.

He could still taste the sickly minibar whisky he'd tried earlier, and see the glass he'd smashed in frustration. He ordered hot chocolate from the automat.

Curiously, his loins stirred when he glimpsed the dried blood on his arm, from the previous attempt at self-harm. He was aroused. He thought of that girl in reception; he could make her submit, easily. All this training, his skills. He could easily overpower her, he could –

Gods, what the hells is wrong with me…?

His hands shook, and his palms felt sweaty. To calm his nerves, he ordered a double-soothe, to be blended with his drink.

His thoughts wandered to the Bureau, their shady dealings and whether they really had anybody's best interests at heart…he found he didn't care, one way or the other, at this point. The concept of right/wrong was a subjective point of view, malleable whichever way the wind blew.

Whether it's the Bureau or their opposite number, each outfit has the same motives, the same means, the same ends, the same victims…so what's the bloody difference?

The newsfeed scrolled to its next story. At first he didn't take much notice, but his link brought it to his attention, nonetheless:

'…and to our recent techo-news. British Aerospatiale concern, Recondite, announced today the successful completion of tests for their new fusion-engine design, heralding the end of their secretive R&D phase at their secure facility in Northamptonshire.

'Industry commentators have remarked how Recondite's expedited development programme had been kept so closely under wraps that surprise was palpable across the markets, which although sluggish to react have nonetheless soared in response, securing

them a place as market leaders, leaving Pan-Asian concern ESL, headquartered in Geneva, trailing in the wind.

'Rumours abound of a theft from ESL's Zug facility that made sensitive design specs available to the open market, but a Recondite spokesperson has assured stakeholders their revolutionary Huldrych fusion-engine has been on the drawing board for some time. This has led to a great deal of industry-wide speculation as to whether ESL in Geneva will ever recover from this crippling set back, or indeed survive as one of the top five market leaders.'

Devin blinked as he disseminated the information.

So the comsat data hadn't been as useless as the Bureau had led him to believe. They'd manoeuvred one of their companies to claim credit…

Why did O'Neill lie to me about it?

He instinctively felt it was another of his repulsive mind-games, designed to keep him off balance and assert control. His hate ossified and he imagined grasping his scrawny neck, squeezing the putrid life out of him.

Intestoration crippled, but Devin held on to his fantasy for a few more sweet moments, his shrieking a blend of pain and sheer frustration.

This cannot go on. How can I live the rest of my life, like this?

The intestoration ebbed. He regained a measure of calm, propped against the windowsill.

I will be free of them. Some day.

The desire was strong, and very real. While there was still something left of himself to save, buried deep in there, somewhere… he had to be free from them.

"Adagio Cantabile." The disturbing newsfeed was overlaid with the second movement of the sonata.

He had to find a way to let go, to relax by some means. But he couldn't shake the determination he must be free of the Bureau. It was hard-wired into him, now.

Maybe one day when conditions were right, he would be. It would only be possible if he had the proper means to disappear, to detune his link so he could 'vanish' once and for all, from their all-pervading immersive web. But he would have to bide his time, until then. Watch and listen, for the right opportunity to present itself.

So, until then…

Well, he supposed that until then…he would be forced to do their bidding.

- THE END -

– ABOUT THE AUTHOR, ABOUT THIS BOOK –

John Patrick Kirk, born and raised in London in the early 1970s, has from a young age held a deep passion for science fiction. At the age of fourteen he was encouraged to write his first novel by his then comprehensive English teacher, Dan McCarthy. It was called 'The Martian God' and got him an A*.

Around the same time, the near-forgotten gem 'Star Cops' was broadcast on BBC2 television and Chris Boucher's writing had a major influence on the burgeoning young author. As John went on to devour the 'hard' sci-fi of Arthur C Clarke, Isaac Asimov, and later Ben Bova, Stephen Baxter, et al, this formed the basis of his self-confessed addiction to the genre that maintains its grip to this very day.

Over the years John also developed a passion for the 'spy-fi' genre through his late father's encouragement to read the original Ian Fleming Bond novels, but John's preference for realism steered him towards a love of the grittier styles of John Le Carré, Adam Hall, and Frederick Forsyth. When he combined all of these influences into a hybrid 'hard-spy/sci-fi' genre, the character Marc Devin was born.

Much like his main protagonist, John began his professional life as a maintenance 'tech which lead to a very satisfying career in Learning & Development and LEAN 6 Sigma, his current vocation of the past 20+ years. He has a daughter and two step-sons, and resides with his wife in Northamptonshire, UK.

Visit the author's website for more information on his books and influences, at:

http://gollancz.wixsite.com/authorjohnkirk

DEVIN's WAY 02: Jupiter's Moon

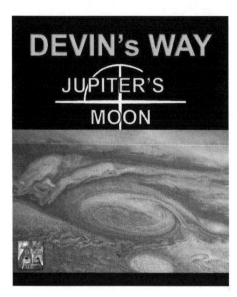

In part II of the Devin's Way trilogy, Marc Devin is adjusting badly to life as an agent of Bureau 09. He has been robbed of his former identity and precious status, and must languish as a lowly 'tech for maintenance contractor 'UniTech'. Luckily for the Bureau and their nefarious schemes, this means that he can literally be anyplace, anytime under the guise of essential maintenance, but unluckily for him this dooms his future to one of filthy crawlspaces, and Gods-forsaken hells-holes.

Amidst reports of valuable consignments disappearing in the Jovian system, Devin is stationed aboard an ice mining platform on the moon Europa to investigate. However he doesn't bank on the outright hostility and paranoia that meets him there, and the mysterious Leviathan that could threaten all of them. But as the game unfolds the truth emerges, and he is shown by the enigmatic Eva Croft how to loosen the reigns of the Bureau and regain some of his sanity before it is too late.

DEVIN's WAY 03: Martian Rising

In part III of the Devin's Way trilogy, 41yr old Marc Devin deals with an old foe at a luxury resort on Earth's Moon, and is sent to Mars to investigate reports of a rumoured 'find' deep in the frozen soil. Such a find would give the Bureau's enemy, the United States of the Americas, dominance in the region, and Devin must either twist the finding into Europa-State's interests or destroy it for good - that's assuming it even exists in the first place!

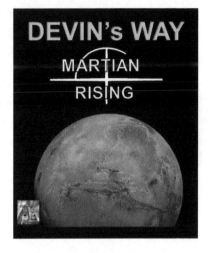

But he doesn't bank on falling for his 'mark', the young woman he is to initially exploit in order to get closer to the find. As he stares death in the face on the unforgiving surface of Mars, will Marc Devin find redemption for his soul and at last discover a way to be free of the Bureau, once and for all?

Printed in Great Britain
by Amazon

34567176R00099